A
Harlequin
Romance

D0733236

OTHER
Harlequin Romances
by ANNE WEALE

Many of these titles are available at your local bookseller,
or through the Harlequin Reader Service.

For a free catalogue listing all available Harlequin Romances,
send your name and address to:

HARLEQUIN READER SERVICE,
M.P.O. Box 707, Niagara Falls, N.Y. 14302
Canadian address: Stratford, Ontario, Canada.

or use order coupon at back of book.

THE FIELDS
OF HEAVEN

by

ANNE WEALE

HARLEQUIN BOOKS   TORONTO
WINNIPEG

Original hard cover edition published in 1973
by Mills & Boon Limited.

© Anne Weale 1973

SBN 373-01747-2

Harlequin edition published January 1974

Printed in Canada

1747

CHAPTER I

THE night before the wedding, Imelda came home from the office to find her mother sitting, white-faced, at the kitchen table, and a stranger, who turned out to be a policewoman in plain clothes, making a pot of tea.

It was not the first time that the local police had brought bad news to Margaret Calthorpe. Nine years earlier, when Imelda was eleven, her father had been killed in a road accident, leaving her mother with a rambling Edwardian house in an unfashionable part of London, three dependent children, and no money.

This time the news was less shocking. The person who had died was Miss Florence Maud Partridge, aged seventy-six, a relation of the late William Calthorpe whom his wife had met only once, long ago, when Imelda was a baby.

"But apparently we are her next of kin, and there are half a dozen cats and two budgerigars being fed by a neighbour until someone arrives to take charge. Oh, dear, this would happen today of all days!" exclaimed Mrs. Calthorpe distractedly.

"Don't worry, Mother. I'll deal with it," Imelda said calmly.

"How can you, darling? It means going to Nor[...] and arranging the funeral, and —"

"I can cope," Imelda assured her. She turned [...] pleasant-faced policewoman. "My mother is getti[...] ried in the morning, and she and my stepfather [...] to Devon for a fortnight. I'm having a day off [...] and I'm sure my boss will let me take Thursd[...]

5

day as well, when I explain the situation. We have friends who will keep an eye on my younger brother and sister for a few days. If I go to Norfolk tomorrow, immediately after the wedding, and stay there till Sunday afternoon, there'll be ample time to sort out everything, don't you think?"

"I should think so, Miss Calthorpe," said the policewoman. "A lot depends on whether Miss Partridge left instructions concerning her property, and the pets. It's always more complicated when people don't make a will. Our only information is that she was taken ill on Saturday, and died in hospital early this morning. At first she didn't wish anyone to be notified, but then she changed her mind and gave this address."

"I had forgotten about her, poor old soul," Mrs. Calthorpe confessed. "She was my husband's mother's elder sister. She kept a queer little shop, and we visited her once on our way to Sheringham for a holiday. She was wearing clothes which must have belonged to her grandmother, and the house was dark and gloomy, and full of stray cats. She was very eccentric even then! "

Soon after the policewoman's departure, the two younger Calthorpes came home with Ben Dereham, their prospective stepfather, who was also John's mathematics master at the local grammar school.

John, who had been eight when his father died, was now a six-foot Sixth-Former. Lucy Calthorpe was fifteen, and as cheerfully scatterbrained as her brother was scholarly.

"Do you think it's suitable for Imelda to go to Norfolk on her own, Ben?" asked Mrs. Calthorpe, having explained what had happened during their absence.

It was the first week of the Easter holidays, and John and Lucy had spent the day helping Ben to move his be-

longings from his flat to their home. Ben was a widower with a married daughter in New Zealand.

"It won't be a pleasant task for her, but I'm sure she will tackle it every bit as efficiently as you or I could," he answered.

"Anyway, you can't cancel your honeymoon on account of some half-dotty old lady you didn't know, Mum," remarked Lucy.

Her mother frowned. "Don't speak callously of her, Lucy. I feel ashamed of forgetting her existence all these years."

That night, when Imelda was reading in bed, her mother came to her room on the top floor of the house. Until recently, the three large bedrooms on the first floor had been occupied by the lodgers whose rents, and Imelda's salary, had formed the family income.

After they had chatted for a while, Mrs. Calthorpe said, "I must go to bed. I really came up to say thank you for being such a wonderful help to me since Daddy died. You're such a sensible creature, Melly dear. I've relied on you too much, probably. It hasn't been fair to take the lion's share of your earnings, and expect you to help with looking after the lodgers."

"It wasn't 'fair' for you to be left alone with the three of us," Imelda said gently. "Now you have Ben to rely on, and I'm planning a grand splurge on clothes," she added, smiling.

After her mother had gone, she switched out the light and lay thinking about the changes which her mother's second marriage would make to her own way of life. As long as she lived at home, she intended to make an appropriate contribution to the household expenses, but it would be lovely to have a larger share of her salary to spend as she pleased.

In spite of her joking remark, a restricted clothes budget had not been her greatest frustration during the years of stringent economy. She liked to be attractively dressed, but she had never spent her lunch hours browsing in boutiques like many girls in their late teens. There were certain shops which lured her, but they were not dress shops. Unbeknown to her family, Imelda had a secret passion; one which now, at long last, she could indulge. As soon as she came back from Norfolk . . .

Anticipating pleasures in store, she fell asleep.

At five o'clock the following afternoon, Imelda stood at the bookstall on Liverpool Street Station, casting her eyes over the colourful display of magazines in search of something to read on the two-hour journey to Norwich. The publication which she chose was an expensive, specialised journal to which she had long wished to subscribe, but had had to be content with studying in the Reading Room at the Public Library

The train was not due to depart until half past five and, being in good time, she found a corner seat in an unoccupied compartment. After stowing her overnight case on the rack, she took off the scarlet peaked cap she had bought for the wedding, and smoothed her straight, mid-brown hair which was held by a tortoiseshell slide at the nape of her neck.

John Calthorpe was fair and clever. Lucy was dark and pretty. I have common sense, thought Imelda, with a rueful grin at her reflection in the mirror below the luggage rack.

In the past, pondering on the different combinations of genes which had caused her to have commonplace hazel eyes instead of Lucy's long-lashed, deep brown ones, and a brain much less brilliant than her brother's, Imelda had

8

reached the conclusion that it would have been a disadvantage for her to have been very clever. With a mind like John's, she would have wanted to go to university, thereby adding to her mother's financial difficulties instead of reducing them by leaving school early and entering a large insurance office. In five years she had graduated from typist to shorthand-typist to senior secretary. Her job was not an exciting one. Often it was rather dull work. But it was well paid which, up to now, had been the main thing.

And now, if I wished, I could change to a different sort of office, she reflected, relaxing in her corner, and thinking of her mother and Ben whose train had left Paddington Station a couple of hours ago.

At this point the carriage door was opened by a slim, well-dressed, white-haired woman who, judging by her lack of luggage, had been to London for the day. She smiled briefly at Imelda as she settled herself in the opposite corner. Then she disappeared behind an evening newspaper. With an unaccustomed and delightful feeling of luxury, Imelda opened her magazine.

Immersed in its pages, she was only dimly aware that the train was crowded to Chelmsford where it disgorged a large number of commuters. At Colchester, she and the woman opposite were left alone in the compartment.

Imelda had not been out of London for ten years. After her father's death, there had been no money to spare for the seaside holidays of her early childhood. As the train sped through rural Suffolk, she let the magazine fall to her lap, and gazed in some wonderment at the April landscape, sprinkled with isolated houses. Living in crowded London, one tended to forget that, in spite of the population explosion and the spreading network of motorways, large parts of provincial England were still green and pleasant.

A steward passed along the corridor, reminding passengers that tea was obtainable in the buffet car. Imelda and the woman opposite rose to their feet at the same moment. As Imelda subsided to allow the older woman to go first, her travelling companion indicated the magazine, and said, "I see you are a collector. So am I. What is your line?"

Rather startled by this unexpected overture, Imelda said frankly, "I can't afford to buy real antiques. I have a small collection of buttonhooks, but they're only 'junk', I'm afraid."

"Not at all. Buttonhooks are charming," answered the woman. "I often have to resist them when I'm hunting for the things which I collect. Shall we introduce ourselves, and have tea together? I'm Elizabeth Wingfield.

"This *is* an unexpected treat," she remarked presently, when they were sharing a table for two in the buffet car. "I love to compare notes, but, living in the depths of Norfolk, I meet very few other collectors. One gossips with dealers, of course, but it isn't quite the same thing. You're not getting off at Ipswich, I hope?"

"I'm going to Norwich."

"Oh, good, then we've plenty of time. Is Norwich your home?"

"No, I live in London. What do you collect, Mrs. Wingfield?"

"My main interest is in antique sewing tools. Do you know the kind of things I mean? Little acorn-shaped thimble cases, and ivory cotton barrels, and pretty mother-of-pearl thread-winders. What I want most of all is a hemming bird, but they are very hard to find. I've been searching for one for several years. Tell me about your buttonhooks. How many have you?"

"Only thirty," Imelda replied. "The hooks with silver handles are usually a pound or more, which has been too expensive for me. I have one folding hook which looks at first glance like a penknife. The handle is engraved mother-of-pearl, and I had to pay seventy pence for it. But most of my collection are steel hooks with slogans stamped on them, and they seldom cost more than ten pence."

"How interesting. What sort of slogans?" asked Mrs. Wingfield.

"Victorian advertising slogans. A common one is 'The Wood-Milne Rubber Heel Pad – Double Comfort and Life of Boots'," Imelda explained.

Some minutes after they returned to the compartment, the ticket collector entered. "Did you know you are in the Second Class, madam?" he asked Mrs. Wingfield, when she surrendered her ticket.

"Yes, I did, thank you, Inspector." When he had gone, she said to Imelda, "This train is less crowded than usual. I find a day in London so tiring nowadays that I generally travel First Class to be sure of a seat. However, as I arrived at Liverpool Street, I caught sight of a woman I know, and she's such a terrible bore. So I came in here to avoid her, and have had the undeserved pleasure of talking to you. The taxi service at the station at Norwich is not as good as it might be. My grandson will be there to meet me. Will you be met, or can we give you a lift, my dear?"

Imelda shook her head. "It's very kind of you, but I think I can catch a bus to where I'm going. It's about fifteen miles outside Norwich."

Mrs. Wingfield looked doubtful. "The country buses are not as frequent as they used to be when fewer people had private cars. Where are you going?"

Imelda told her, and Mrs. Wingfield exclaimed. "But we live only two miles from there. I shouldn't dream of leaving you to wait for the bus."

The train was a long one, and they were in a rear carriage, which gave them a long walk down the platform when the train arrived at Thorpe Station.

"Ah, I can see Charles," said Mrs. Wingfield, with a pleased expression, as they approached the barrier. "Oh . . . Beatrix is with him," she added.

The tall, dark man who bent to kiss her cheek, and take her parcels, was older than Imelda had anticipated. She had expected the grandson to be about twenty. This man was thirty or more. She was mistaken also in taking the woman for his wife.

Mrs. Wingfield introduced her as Mrs. Otley, and added, "Beatrix is an antique dealer, but she sells fine furniture and porcelain, no Victoriana or bits and pieces such as I collect." She turned to her grandson. "Miss Calthorpe is going in our direction, and is not being met, so I've offered her a lift with us."

"By all means," he replied, with stiff politeness. "Let me take your bag for you, Miss Calthorpe."

His unsmiling courtesy was in marked contrast to the warmth of his grandmother's personality. Mrs. Otley, too, struck Imelda as rather aloof. She was dressed with casual elegance and emanated an expensive French fragrance which was more noticeable in the car.

A glimpse of a Norman castle was the only memorable detail of Imelda's first impression of Norwich. When they had left the city behind, Mrs. Wingfield broke off a conversation with her grandson, and turned to look at Imelda who was sitting behind him.

"Where exactly are you staying, Miss Calthorpe? We know most people in our part of the county. Possibly we know your friends."

"I'm going to stay at Miss Partridge's house. The Miss Partridge who died in hospital yesterday."

12

For some seconds there was a hush. Then, unexpectedly, since she had been sitting in silence, not troubling to make any polite small-talk, Mrs. Otley said, "Do you mean that extraordinary old person who owns the shop full of dust and cobwebs and mice droppings? I didn't know she was dead. Are you a relation?"

"Miss Partridge was my father's aunt. I never knew her," said Imelda.

"But, my dear child, you can't mean to stay there," exclaimed Mrs. Wingfield. "I've known Miss Partridge for years, since her mother was alive. In those days the house was spotless. But now! – You can't possibly sleep there. Heaven knows what a state it must be in."

"I expect there's a pub, isn't there? Or perhaps the neighbour will put me up. The one who is taking care of the cats."

"That will be Bessie Medlar," said Mrs. Wingfield. "I don't think she has a spare room, and none of our three public houses does bed and breakfast any more. It's a very *small* market town, you see, and too near to Norwich to need a hotel of its own. Never mind: you must spend the night with us."

Imelda began to protest that she could not impose on them, but Mrs. Wingfield brushed aside her objections, and assured her that they always kept a room ready for an unexpected guest, and would be delighted to have her.

"You say you never knew Miss Partridge?" remarked Mrs. Otley.

"The last time my parents saw her, I was a baby. My father is dead, and it's impossible for my mother to come to Norfolk at present, so I'm here to see about the funeral, and to find homes for the cats," explained Imelda.

"Are there no other relations?"

13

"Not as far as I know."

"We're nearly there," said Mrs. Wingfield. "Would you like to look at the house tonight, or would it be better to wait until tomorrow morning?"

"There's little point in stopping now. There's no electric light in the place, and the oil lamps may not be working. The old girl was reputed to go to bed before it was dark," said Charles Wingfield.

His tone had a briskness which might be characteristic, but which made Imelda suspect that not only was he thinking of his evening meal, but that he felt his grandmother was too quick to offer hospitality to strangers.

"Yes, you're right. I'd forgotten that," agreed Mrs. Wingfield. "But slow down as we go past, Charles, so that Miss Calthorpe can at least see the place."

Imelda's introduction to her great-aunt's property was a daunting sight at the end of a long, tiring day. The small town – a mere village, to a Londoner's eyes – was an unplanned conglomeration of the building styles of several centuries. The bank and the chemist's shop were next door to each other in a Georgian terrace. A butcher and a hairdresser had premises in a row of thatched cottages, and the Post Office was a red brick Edwardian villa. The late Miss Partridge had lived in a small, double-fronted house with an almost indecipherable fascia board above the bow window to the right of the shabby front door. The house was separated from the busy main road only by the width of the pavement, and the light from the nearby street lamp showed that the panes of the downstairs windows were begrimed by a long accumulation of summer dust and winter wet flung up by the wheels of passing traffic. The upper windows were veiled by Nottingham lace curtains which, even from a distance, looked as if they had not been washed for five or ten years.

"It looks rather eerie, doesn't it?" remarked Mrs. Wingfield, in the few minutes that the car was at a standstill on the opposite side of the road. "But early Victorian houses are usually very solidly built. I daresay that, cleaned and painted, it would look altogether different."

"It needs more than paint to make it habitable," said Beatrix Otley. "When I first came here, I made some enquiries about it. It has not been modernised since it was built. There's a privy at the bottom of the garden."

At this point, Charles Wingfield took his foot off the brake and drove on. By now the spring dusk had deepened into darkness, and as far as Imelda could judge they drove another two or three miles by way of minor roads before he swung the car between two tall brick gateposts surmounted by weathered stone urns. Inside the gateway was a lodge house with a small white-fenced garden and picket gate. Here he stopped the car, and climbed out and walked round to open the door for Mrs. Otley.

"Goodnight, Elizabeth. Goodnight, Miss Calthorpe," she said.

Her parting was warmer than her greeting which had been noticeably off-hand, Imelda remembered.

"The Lodge used to be my home," said Mrs. Wingfield, while her grandson escorted Mrs. Otley to her front door, and waited while she found her latchkey. "I was sorry to have to leave it. Small houses are so much cosier than large ones. The Hall, as you will see in a moment, is a delightful old house. But it was designed to be run by at least half a dozen servants, and nowadays people in the country are lucky if they have one good daily help. We are extremely fortunate to have a couple. Mrs. Betts cooks, and Mr. Betts does a bit of everything. Goodness knows how we should manage if they retired. You see, my elder grandson and his wife were in an appalling air disaster

15

three years ago. So Charles and I have joined forces to keep the place up until Henry, my *great*-grandson, is old enough to take over."

By now it was apparent to Imelda that Mrs. Wingfield must be considerably older than her trim figure and energetic appearance suggested, and that although social changes might make it impossible to staff the Hall in the manner of former times, the family still enjoyed a life style much grander than that to which the Calthorpes were accustomed.

From the Lodge, the drive passed through open parkland for some distance, and then curved round the edge of a small wood. For an instant the headlights illuminated the graceful façade of a Queen Anne manor house. As the car crunched to a halt on the gravelled sweep, the front door was flung open and three children burst from the house. The smallest, a girl of not more than six, was wearing pyjamas and clasping a large teddy bear. They were followed by a stout, middle-aged woman to whom, after she had hugged the children, Mrs. Wingfield said, "Have they been good, Mrs. Betts? What are we having for supper? Something elastic, I hope. Miss Calthorpe is spending the night with us."

"Good evening, miss." Mrs. Betts gave Imelda a friendly nod. "It's my steak and kidney pudding tonight, madam. With Mr. Charles being out all day, I thought he'd be glad of something substantial this evening."

"Yes, indeed. We shall all enjoy it." Mrs. Wingfield fondled the ears of a grey-muzzled, elderly labrador which had been waiting, tail thrashing, for a share of her attention. "Hello, Poppy, old girl."

Charles had disappeared. After unlocking the boot, and instructing the children to take charge of Imelda's

16

light case and his grandmother's parcels, he had driven the car to its garage somewhere behind the house.

About twenty minutes later, when Imelda had just finished tidying herself in a bedroom papered and curtained with red and white *toile de Jouy*, and furnished with walnut chests which she judged to have been made for the Hall's first occupants, ten-year-old Henry came to show her the way to a small sitting-room at the back of the house.

"My sisters have gone to bed now. I stay up till nine in the holidays," he told her.

His uncle did not reappear until the two women, sherry glasses in hand, were on their way to the dining-room. While Henry attended to his great-grandmother, Charles drew out the chair on which Imelda was to sit.

The children had had high tea at six. "Can I watch TV?" Henry asked his uncle. "Mrs. Betts says it's okay with her."

"Yes, for an hour. But don't let me catch you at it after quarter to nine," Charles warned him.

"The Betts have a television set, but Charles and I prefer other relaxations in the evening," said Mrs. Wingfield to Imelda. "He reads, when he's free of the paperwork which bedevils modern farming, and I do canvas work – popularly known as 'tapestry'."

"Do you sew, Miss Calthorpe?" asked Charles.

It was so obvious that his question was a perfunctory politeness, and that he had no interest in whether she sewed, or in anything else about her, that Imelda felt a flash of irritation. If he could not conceal his indifference, it would be better to ignore her.

"I sometimes make clothes for myself and my younger sister. I'm not a skilled needlewoman," she answered.

17

"Embroidery is a plum to reserve for one's middle years," said Mrs. Wingfield. "I didn't take up my needle until I was forty."

The second course, a fresh fruit salad, was on the table before Charles felt it necessary to address another remark to Imelda.

"I think you are optimistic in hoping to find homes for Miss Partridge's collection of cats. It's difficult to persuade people to take kittens, and full-grown animals are less appealing," he said. "Your best course would be to have the whole lot put down."

"Perhaps." Her tone was non-committal.

As he poured cream on his fruit, she glanced at him again. He reminded her of a picture of the Duke of Wellington on the wall of John's bedroom. But where her brother's hero had had blue eyes and a high colour, Charles Wingfield's eyes were light grey, and his skin was tanned rather than ruddy, suggesting a recent skiing holiday. But his large, high-bridged nose was extremely Wellingtonian, and there was something about his mouth which made her suspect that, in spite of finding *her* uninteresting, where women in general were concerned, he might share the Iron Duke's propensities. Probably the type who appealed to him was a glamorous Amazon, almost as tall as himself, for whom hunting, sailing and roaring round the county in a fast car were life's greatest pleasures.

"If you'll excuse me, I'll take my coffee to the library. I have some rather urgent letters to write," said Charles, at the end of the meal.

When he had gone, his grandmother said, "Would you care to see my collection? As Charles has retired to his sanctum, let's take our coffee to mine, shall we?"

Mrs. Wingfield's antique sewing tools were housed in two glass-topped tables in her sitting-room upstairs. "This

18

is really a bedroom, but I had so many belongings which I didn't wish to leave at the Lodge when we decided to let it that I converted this room into my private parlour, and I sleep next door in the dressing-room," she explained. "The tables are not locked. Do open them and take out anything which interests you. Sophie and Fanny often do, and nothing has ever been damaged."

She put on a pair of spectacles, and sat down at a table on which a piece of half finished canvas work was stretched on a beechwood frame. "I shall 'whistle and ride' as they say in Norfolk. Embroidery doesn't call for hours of leisure, as so many people seem to think. The secret is to do a little every day."

For the next half an hour her needle flew back and forth through the canvas while Imelda pored over the tools, asking questions about the objects she did not recognise. One of the tables held tools made of ivory, bone and nacre, and the other contained those made of wood, brass and tartan ware.

She was peering at five views of Coventry through a minute lens, smaller than a grain of rice, in the end of a carved bone needle-case, when a tap at the door was followed by Charles's reappearance.

"I'm taking Poppy as far as the post," he told his grandmother. He turned to Imelda. "Shouldn't you telephone your people, Miss Calthorpe? In view of your rather vague ideas about where you might spend the night, they must be a trifle anxious, I should have thought."

"Yes, do ring up your home, Imelda," urged Mrs. Wingfield, her pleasant tone leavening the bite of sarcasm in his. "Charles will show you where the phone is."

"You will have to dial 0. We're not on STD here yet," he said, when they were downstairs. On the point of turning away, he checked and studied her for a moment. "You seem very young to be sent on an errand of this nature. How old are you?"

"I'm twenty. How old are you, Mr. Wingfield?" she retorted.

"Too old to embark on a journey without making sure of suitable accommodation when I reached my destinaion," he replied sardonically. Followed by the old black bitch, which had been lying on a rug patiently waiting, he let himself out of the front door.

Had it not been for upsetting Mrs. Wingfield, with whom in spite of the great difference in their ages she felt a strong rapport, and also for the fact that two or three miles of unlighted country roads separated the Hall from the town, Imelda would have sought shelter at the nearest police station – anywhere rather than spend the night under Charles Wingfield's roof.

She managed to keep her vexation out of her voice during a brief conversation with her brother. John said that, a few minutes earlier, he had been talking to their mother and Ben, now far away in Devon.

After the call, Imelda waited for the operator to tell her how much it had cost, and then she ran upstairs to fetch the necessary coins from her bag, and put them beside the telephone.

"I hope your mother's anxiety was not redoubled on hearing that you were staying with strangers," said Mrs. Wingfield, when Imelda returned.

Imelda explained why her mother was also away from home that night.

"Good gracious! No wonder you look tired, my dear. If I were you, I should go to bed. Would you care for a hot drink to help you to sleep in a strange bed? I can soon make one for you." She opened a cupboard, revealing an electric kettle and the provisions for various types of nightcaps. "I always have a cup of hot chocolate to make me drowsy."

"No, thank you – and thank you again for being so very kind to me."

"You are most welcome. Goodnight, child. Sleep well."

In her room, Imelda discovered that there was nothing a guest might want which had not been provided. A vacuum flask of iced water, and an airtight tin of biscuits, stood on the bedside table. There were books on some hanging shelves, tissues beside the eighteenth-century dressing mirror and, in the adjoining bathroom, an expanding line which could be stretched across the bath alcove so that guests might wash and drip dry such things as tights. The final addition to her comfort was to find, when she climbed into bed, that although the house was centrally heated, a hot water bottle had been placed between the sheets.

When Imelda woke up and looked at her watch, she was dismayed to find it was eight o'clock. At home, an alarm clock woke her at seven, and she had hoped habit would rouse her at about the same time this morning.

It was twenty minutes before she was ready to go downstairs. Shortly before she left her room, she heard children's voices below her window, and glanced out to see the three young Wingfields running across the lawn towards the fence which kept the ivory-coloured cattle grazing the park from invading the pleasure gardens. All three children were wearing navy jerseys with fudge corduroy trousers tucked into gumboots, for the grass was silvery-grey with heavy dew.

There was so much to admire in the house that the night before she had overlooked the mezzotints on the staircase wall. As she paused, half way down the stairs, unable to resist a closer look at an eighteenth-century picnic scene entitled "The Angler's Repast", she heard the rustle of a newspaper, and Charles Wingfield's voice asking, "How long is Miss Whatsit staying here?"

"She has to return to London on Sunday," was Mrs. Wingfield's answer. "You seem very hostile towards her. Why? I think she's a nice girl."

"I wouldn't say I was hostile. It's merely that I have enough on my plate without being involved in old Miss Partridge's obsequies."

"You haven't been asked to involve yourself, my dear."

"No, but Miss Thingummy doesn't impress me as being too competent, and as you'll be out all day she may think she can turn to me when she can't cope."

"Considering your marked lack of amiability towards her, I don't think you need fear that," was the dry reply.

"I daresay she's only come down here for what she hopes to get out of it. She admits that it's years since her family had anything to do with the old girl. It's amazing how distant relations appear on the scene at the sniff of a legacy. But I think she'll be disappointed if she's expecting to find a fat stocking hidden under Miss Partridge's mattress."

"You're too cynical, Charles. I'm sure that's not why she's here."

"You're too trusting, Granny." Imelda heard a short laugh. "If Miss Partridge had any money, which I doubt, she's probably left it to those fleabitten cats of hers." The newspaper rustled, and there was silence.

Realising that the solid wood door of the dining-room must be an inch or two ajar for her to have overheard this conversation, Imelda was forced to remain on the stairs for some minutes. Her embarrassment at being an unintentional eavesdropper on an exchange which certainly bore out the adage that listeners never heard good of themselves was secondary to her intense resentment of Charles's contemptuous assessment of her character.

"Good morning. I'm sorry I'm late," she said, as she entered the dining-room.

Mrs. Wingfield put aside the letter she had been reading, and took off her spectacles. "Good morning. How did you sleep?"

"Very well, thank you." With a brisk "Good morning" to Charles, who had risen to his feet, Imelda took her place at the table.

"I'll have the coffee pot refilled, and tell Mrs. Betts you're down," he said. "What would you like for breakfast, Miss ... er ... Calthorpe? We had bacon and eggs, but perhaps you would prefer a boiled egg?"

"I'll have cornflakes, if I may?" said Imelda, turning to Mrs. Wingfield. She had noticed several packets of cereals on the Sheraton sideboard.

"Help yourself, my dear," said her hostess. While her grandson was fetching fresh coffee, she added, "Unfortunately I have to attend a Women's Institute conference today, Imelda. I'll drop you at Miss Partridge's house on my way to Norwich, and pick you up on my way home, about five o'clock. I wish I could help you to deal with everything, but I think Sergeant Saxtead at the Police Station will be the best person to turn to if you find yourself at a loss. He's a very nice man who has been in this area for several years."

Perhaps he will know of someone who will put me up as a p.g. for the rest of my time here, thought Imelda. Aloud, she said, "Yes, the policewoman who came to tell us about Great-Aunt Florence said the local police would do their best to help me with any problems."

When Charles returned to the dining-room, he said, "I'd better be off. Would you care for the paper, Miss Calthorpe?" He placed the local morning newspaper on the table at her elbow.

As he bent to kiss Mrs. Wingfield's cheek, Imelda thought, How would you like it, I wonder, if anyone suggested that you are only attentive to your grandmother in the hope of being her legatee?

"I'll see you both this evening." With a glance at Imelda which held, she felt, a sardonic glint, he snapped his fingers as a signal to the recumbent labrador, and they both left the room.

You definitely won't see me again, Imelda resolved.

Before she departed for the city, Mrs. Wingfield introduced Imelda to Miss Partridge's next door neighbour, Mrs. Bessie Medlar.

"Well, miss, I in't a-saying you in't related to Miss Partridge. But my instructions from the police sergeant was not to let nobody in the house, do they might take something," remarked this old body, eyeing Imelda with keenest interest. "Do you send them up to see me, Mrs. Medlar, he say to me."

"Did it occur to you to bring some sort of identification, Imelda?" asked Mrs. Wingfield, as they drove to the police station which she had to pass on her way to the city.

"Yes, Ben – my stepfather – said I should need something. I have my own birth certificate, the certificate of my mother's first marriage, and my father's papers as well."

"Ah, yes, I've been expecting you, Miss Calthorpe," said Sergeant Saxtead, when Imelda presented herself to him. "If you don't mind waiting for a few minutes, I'll run you down to the house and you can have a look round

24

for any papers the old lady may have left. You might be a little bit nervous in there on your own. It's very old-fashioned – and very neglected! The cats have kept the mice and rats away, but there are plenty of spiders about, and cockroaches too, I shouldn't wonder."

Far from being the middle-aged country bobby she had visualised, Sergeant Saxtead was young, good-looking, and no more countrified than Imelda.

"You spent last night in Norwich, I expect?" he said, as he started the police car.

Imelda explained about meeting Mrs. Wingfield on the train, and being invited to stay at the Hall.

"She's a very nice person, Mrs. Wingfield," he said. "She told you what happened to her grandchildren's parents, I suppose?"

"About the air crash? Yes, she did."

"It happened just after I came here. They've had several tragedies in that family. Mrs. Wingfield lost both her sons in the last war, and her husband died earlier than he would have done if he hadn't been badly wounded at the start of the 1914–18 lot. Trying to find out if Miss Partridge had any relations reminds me that it was quite a job to contact Mr. Charles Wingfield after his brother and sister-in-law were killed. Eventually he was traced to an island in the Mediterranean."

"What was he doing there?"

"I couldn't say. He'd been all over the place before he had to come back and take charge at the Hall. A bit of a rolling stone, by all accounts." With an abruptness which suggested that he felt he had been indiscreet, the Sergeant changed the subject.

Imelda *was* glad of his company the first time she entered the late Miss Partridge's home.

"Have you ever read *Great Expectations*, Sergeant?"

25

she asked, as they stood side by side in the musty-smelling gloom of her great-aunt's sitting-room.

"No, but I saw the film," he answered. "You're thinking of Miss Haversham who was jilted at the church and was still wearing her white dress and veil years later. I remember the scene where the mice were scuttling about on the table among the remains of the wedding breakfast. Yes, I thought of *Great Expectations* when I first came in here.

"The majority of old people are very concerned about their funeral expenses," he went on. "However hard up they may be, they nearly always have an insurance policy, or some money put by in the house. There's none here that I can find, and the old dear next door – who misses nothing! – says she never saw an insurance man calling on Miss Partridge. Or anyone else, for that matter. But your great-aunt was still active, and she went to Norwich regularly once a month. She may have paid her premiums there, and there may be a policy, and a will, hidden away somewhere in here. I've looked in all the obvious places, and in some less obvious ones that we and thieves get to know about. But I haven't found even her pension book, and it wasn't among the effects which she had with her in hospital. Have you any suggestions, Miss Calthorpe?"

"Have you looked in the secret drawer in the writing slope?"

"No. Where's that?" he asked, puzzled.

On a table covered with a cloth of maroon chenille there was a Victorian writing slope, open, and in better repair than most of the slopes Imelda had seen. The green velvet on the hinged leaves was in good condition, and the glass inkwells were still in place. There were even some pens and pencils in the tip-up channel designed for them.

"Not all slopes have secret drawers," she said, removing the various other objects which cluttered the table top. "But this one has –" as she pressed the catch which released a spring which pushed out a drawer in the base of the box.

"Well, I'm damned!" exclaimed the Sergeant. "You are a clever girl. How did you know it was there—"

"My hobby is poking about in junk shops, and one often comes across old writing slopes. They're usually very cheap because they aren't as useful as other kinds of old boxes," she explained, removing Miss Partridge's papers from their hiding place.

Among them, on a single sheet of foolscap, was a carbon copy of her great-aunt's will, made nineteen years ago. It was a brief document. Miss Partridge had bequeathed "all my property, both real and personal, whatsoever and wheresoever, unto my said great-niece, Imelda Jane Calthorpe." Attached to the copy by a rusty berry pin was the letterheading of a firm of Norwich solicitors.

By half past twelve, Imelda had made arrangements for her great-aunt to be buried in the same grave as her parents in the local churchyard early on Saturday morning. She had also made an appointment to see Miss Partridge's solicitor the following day; and, on the recommendation of Sergeant Saxtead, she had arranged to spend the next three nights with Mrs. Walsham, a widow who lived in a neat bungalow on a private housing estate on the fringe of the town.

She had returned from her interview with Mrs. Walsham, and was thinking of going out in search of the town's fish and chip shop, when someone rapped on the back door. It was not Mrs. Medlar, as she expected. It was Beatrix Otley, carrying a small wicker hamper.

27

"Hello," she said, smiling. "I met Charles, and heard that Elizabeth is in Norwich all day. So I thought you might be glad of a lunch basket, and perhaps a sympathetic ear. How are things going?"

"Come inside," said Imelda. "This is very kind of you, Mrs. Otley."

"Don't be formal. Call me Beatrix. What's your name?"

"Imelda. Everywhere is very dirty. Mind you don't spoil your clothes."

Beatrix was wearing flared camel pants with a matching sweater. The broad belt resting loosely on her sleek hips was joined by a huge gilt clasp. "I see what you mean," she remarked, as she followed Imelda to the sitting-room, the least sordid room in the house. "Where are the famous cats? How many are there? Rumour says about twenty."

"Mrs. Medlar next door says only seven. They seem to live in the back bedroom, although there were only two on the bed when we looked in there."

"We?"

"The local police officer, whose escort I was rather relieved to have when I first set foot in here."

"Oh, I see." Beatrix began to unpack the basket. "Have you found out yet who inherits everything?"

"Unless a new will comes to light, apparently I do."

"What on earth will you do with it? Sell it?"

"I suppose so. I haven't had much time to think yet."

The lunch which Beatrix had provided was much nicer than a packet of fish and chips. It began with hot soup from a flask, followed by salmon salad on a bed of cold savoury rice. For pudding there were lemon sorbets produced from an insulated bag, and the picnic ended with cheese and biscuits, and coffee from another flask.

"That was absolutely delicious," Imelda said gratefully. "How is it that you're not at your antique shop today?"

"Oh, Elizabeth told you about it, did she? Today is early closing day in Norwich, and there are very few people about the city. I leave my assistant to cope. Usually I drive round the county on Thursdays, looking for new stock. Genuine antiques are increasingly difficult to find. There's a great deal of junk, but I only deal in the best."

"Yes, so Mrs. Wingfield told me."

"Nevertheless I do have one or two contacts in the junk world. If you wished, I could put you in touch with someone who would clear all this rubbish for you," said Beatrix, with a gesture which encompassed a case of stuffed birds, a Parian figure and a text in a black Oxford frame.

"I agree *that* is rather charmless," said Imelda, eyeing the text. "But would you consider this rubbish?" She picked up a posy container made of pale blue pressed glass in the form of a basket. It had caught her eye earlier, and she had not been surprised to find a tiny raised peacock's head mark on the base of the pot. She handed it to the older woman, who examined it briefly – but not so briefly that she missed the mark, Imelda noted.

Beatrix said, "No doubt, at a jumble sale, this would appeal to a member of a flower arrangement club. But it can't have cost more than a shilling when it was made, and that's all it's really worth now. It's a very crude little ornament to anyone who recognises and appreciates quality."

Imelda waited for her to add something like – "But of course the true value and the current market price are not always related. A number of people collect Sowerby glass nowadays, and therefore this piece might cost two

29

or three pounds, or even more, in a curio shop."

But Beatrix said nothing of the sort, and Imelda found it hard to believe that dealers in the highest class of antiques did not have a shrewd idea of the value of the more humble relics of the past. And surely if Beatrix did know, and assumed that Imelda did not, it would have been helpful to say, "Almost everything which was made more than fifty years ago is a collector's item. So don't part with anything too hastily. One man's rubbish may be another man's treasure trove."

The unpleasant suspicion crept into Imelda's mind that perhaps Beatrix's gesture in bringing the lunch hamper had not been one of disinterested kindness. Perhaps it had been what her mother called "a sprat to catch a mackerel".

After Beatrix had gone, she locked the house and went down the street to the draper's where she bought a nylon overall and two dusters. At the grocery-cum-ironmonger's shop, she bought other cleaning materials. Then she returned to the house and, wearing the overall in place of her good navy dress, she began a systematic inspection.

By mid-afternoon she was very dirty, but convinced that, in spite of its derelict state, her inheritance was not merely a graveyard of white elephants. A wild idea was beginning to shape in her mind.

About four, Mrs. Medlar invited her next door for a cup of tea, and Imelda was able to wash her hands in hot water. She indulged the old lady's desire to gossip for half an hour, and then she went back to the house and, while her hands were clean, she wrapped certain things she had found. She knew they would delight Mrs. Wingfield, and she wanted to give them to her as a token of gratitude for her kindness.

One was a globe-shaped wooden wool-holder decorated with a view of Victorian Ramsgate, and the other was a bone needlecase in the shape of a furled parasol.

It was only a quarter to five when there was another knock at the door. Thinking Mrs. Wingfield must be back earlier than she had expected, Imelda opened the back door and found herself looking up at Charles.

"My grandmother has been delayed. She telephoned from Norwich to ask me to fetch you." Seeing the duster covering her hair, and the dust-begrimed state of her face and arms, he raised an eyebrow and remarked, "You'll be glad of a bath, I should think. What have you been doing?"

"Hunting about to see what's of value, and what's not. What else would you expect me to be doing?" she enquired, in a hard voice. "I won't ask you in, if you don't mind. But if you'll wait a minute there's a package for you to take for Mrs. Wingfield." Quickly she fetched the parcel. "It's for her collection," she told him. "Would you tell her that I'm grateful for her kindness, but that I can't impose on her – or on you – any longer, so I've found someone who will take me as a lodger until I go back to London."

"Who is that?" he asked, looking surprised.

"I shouldn't think you would know her. She's also a Londoner, and she hasn't been living here long."

"I see." He glanced down at the cat which was sidling round his ankles. "Is this a member of Miss Partridge's menagerie?"

"I expect so, but it may not be. Before I take your advice, it would be as well to make certain that the cats to be destroyed were my great-aunt's, and not other people's pets, don't you think?"

His light grey eyes narrowed a little. "Is it because of that advice that you dislike me, Miss Calthorpe?"

31

She had hoped he would recognise her antagonism, but she had not expected him to refer to it. "What makes you think that, Mr. Wingfield?"

"Masculine intuition." There was a hint of amusement in his tone.

She wondered suddenly what he was like when he exerted himself to charm a woman. His deep flexible voice was one of his assets. It was one of those unusual voices which, once heard, are instantly recognisable on the telephone or on tape.

"These mutual antipathies happen sometimes," she said coolly. "Would you excuse me? I have a great deal to do in my few days here." She closed the door and stood in the twilight of the passage, listening to his retreating footsteps. She was shaking slightly. She was not used to being unpleasant to people. Now that the exchange was over, she regretted showing her dislike of him. It might blight her friendship with his grandmother.

What friendship? she thought. I'm going back to London on Sunday.

But at the back of her mind the crazy idea was gaining ground.

Imelda spent Thursday evening listening to the woes of Mrs. Walsham who, after a busy lifetime in a London flat, found herself, at the age of fifty-four, alone and insufficiently occupied in a place which was utterly different from the home she had left, and to which she longed to return.

"I never wanted to come here, but George had set his heart on a nice little place in the country, with a proper garden, and I wanted him to be happy," she explained, watching Imelda eat an excellent mixed grill. "It was all right while he was alive. We moved in a year ago this month, and the weather was lovely last year. We went for drives to the coast, and George set out the garden while I made the place nice indoors. Then in October George died. What with the shock, and not knowing a soul round here except to say Good Morning and Good Evening, and the worry about how to manage on less money – well, sometimes I felt I couldn't go on."

"Have you any children, Mrs. Walsham?"

"Oh, yes, dear – three! But my eldest boy and his family are in Australia, and Betty, my girl, lives in Leeds, and Ron is in the Regular Army. He's stationed in Germany at present. While George was alive I never minded the three of them not living near us. I think it's only when a couple don't get on too well that a woman gets possessive about her children."

She removed Imelda's empty plate, and replaced it with a lavish helping of date pudding and custard. "You don't know how nice it is to have someone to talk to, and cook for." Suddenly she plumped down in the chair on the other side of the table and began to cry. "I'm sorry . . . oh, dear, what must you think of me?" she muttered, fumbling in the pocket of her apron for a handkerchief.

Imelda jumped up and put an arm round her shoulders. "I know how you feel. The same thing happened to my mother, except that she hadn't just moved when my father was killed. But I'm sure you'll make friends here in time, Mrs. Walsham. Have you thought of joining the Women's Institute?"

Mrs. Walsham pulled herself together. "What a silly thing I am, spoiling your meal. I'm all right now. Don't let the custard go cold, dear. Yes, the police sergeant's wife suggested the W.I. But it's only one afternoon a month, and really I need a more regular interest. I saw in the local paper that they're crying out for people to take in university students, and that would have suited me well. But here I'm too far out of Norwich. You can't find a lodger round here, and there aren't many jobs about either, not for women of my age. I wouldn't mind being in a shop. Not all day. Part-time would suit me."

"I'm thinking of opening a shop here," said Imelda, on impulse.

"Are you? What sort of shop?"

"An antique shop . . . well, *bric-à-brac* really."

Mrs. Walsham pursed her lips in doubt. "I don't think you'd find many customers about here. They call it a town, but to my mind it's only a village. People living in Council houses don't usually go in for antiques, and on this estate they like new things. There's seldom a day that I don't see a furniture van delivering to one of these houses. It's all on the H.P., no doubt. George and I always paid cash, so at least I've no debts hanging over me." She rose to put on the kettle. "The man at the shop where I buy my groceries says business is going from bad to worse. It's the supermarkets that's doing it. People go to Norwich to see what's on offer at the supermarkets. I think it would be a mistake to open an antique shop here, dear."

"Antique shops are not like other shops," said Imelda. "Most of one's business is done with 'the trade' – other dealers – and only a little with private customers."

But Mrs. Walsham remained dubious and, lying wakeful in bed long past midnight, Imelda shared her misgivings. In the small hours, the idea which had taken hold of her during the afternoon seemed a hare-brained project.

At breakfast, hearing that Imelda was bound for Norwich, Mrs. Walsham asked if she might go with her. She chatted throughout the bus journey to the city, and Imelda said Yes and No at appropriate moments, while gazing out of the window at the immense Norfolk skyscape which,

34

to her eyes, was as strange and interesting as the scenery of a foreign country.

Had she been alone, she would have liked to listen to the conversation of the two countrywomen in the seats behind them. Talking to Bessie Medlar had aroused her interest in the local dialect with its curious use of "do" in place of "or", and such turns of phrase as "chance time" instead of "occasionally".

"You will sell the property, I presume?" said her great-aunt's solicitor, during her talk with him.

"I haven't made up my mind yet. I'm debating about opening an antique shop."

"Are you engaged in the antique business in London?"

"No, at present I work for an insurance company."

"You have no experience of antiques?"

"No direct experience, but I learned a great deal about the trade from an old man who had been a dealer."

"Have you any capital, Miss Calthorpe?"

"No, none, but —"

"I wouldn't advise starting a business without any capital behind you." The solicitor's smile reminded Imelda of the expression on grown-up faces when a small boy said his ambition was to be a jet pilot, or a little girl announced plans to be a ballerina.

Mrs. Walsham was waiting for her downstairs. "What did he think of your shop idea?"

"He thought it would be most unwise."

"I'm sure he knows best, dear."

There was time to walk about the city before returning to the bus station.

"There's a shop up this street which would interest you," said Mrs. Walsham, as they turned a corner. "I should think it's very expensive. There are no prices on

35

anything, which is usually a sign that they're not afraid to charge, isn't it?"

She led Imelda to a window where the display was made up of a set of Dutch marquetry chairs, and a pair of porcelain candlesticks on a satinwood card table. A number of small but costly objects including snuff boxes, vinaigrettes, silver caddy spoons and porcelain scent bottles were set out on a three-tier dumb waiter. The display was completed by a marine painting on the wall behind the table, a Caucasian rug on the floor, and a beautiful arrangement of flowers.

"This is much, much grander than the sort of shop I had in mind," said Imelda. A thought struck her. "I wonder if this could be –" She stepped backwards to see the name of the business, and was not surprised to read *Beatrix Otley – Antiques and Objets d'Art*.

It was only because they happened to pass the local office of the company which employed her that Imelda suddenly realised there had been no house insurance policy among Miss Partridge's papers. Chiding herself for such an unbusinesslike oversight, she entered the building and remedied the deficiency.

Mrs. Walsham offered to spend the afternoon helping her at the house, but by the time they had had lunch together, Imelda felt the need of some solitude in which to ponder her future.

Clad in her overall and duster, she was standing on a chair in the pantry to see what was on the top shelves, when she heard the creak of the back gate, and masculine footsteps on the flagstones.

Charles Wingfield? Imelda climbed down from the chair feeling unaccountably nervous. But it was not Charles who was crouched down, stroking a cat, when she opened the door.

36

It was a young man in jeans and an ex-Army camouflage jacket. "Hello," he said. "I'm Sam Mutford. I heard old Miss Partridge was dead, so I came round to see if you wanted the place cleared out."

As he rose, he had picked up the cat and now was cradling it on one arm and rubbing it under its chin with his other hand, a treatment which caused ecstatic purring.

"I could do without so many cats. You can take them away if you like," said Imelda, straight-faced.

Sam Mutford grinned, "You'll be lucky!"

His hair was shaggy but clean, and he had a brigand's moustache drooping down at the sides of his mouth. Round his neck he wore a pink scarf pulled through a ring. Because he was fair and blue-eyed, he looked a cross between a Viking and a gypsy.

"That news travelled fast," said Imelda. "Where did you hear it?"

"I live around here."

"You're a dealer?"

"I'm making a start. My dad's in the scrap business, but I'm in the general line. So if there's anything you want to get rid of . . ."

"Have you got a shop?"

He shook his head. Echoing the solicitor, he said, "You need money to set up a shop. I'll have one later, maybe. For the time being I've just got the van."

On some hanging shelves in the passage there was a late Victorian ornament which Imelda would have expected to fetch about a pound if she took it to a back-street dealer. It would not interest a smart shop, like Beatrix Otley's establishment.

She showed it to him. "How much would you give me for that?"

He examined it for damage. At present his hands were

as grimy as hers, but she had the impression that he scrubbed his nails after work. They were short but not bitten. His fingers were not stained with nicotine, and he wore no cheap flashy rings.

"You're from London, I hear," he remarked. "Prices are different up there. You might get more for this, or less there. Those that sell high don't always buy high. I'll give you fifty pence for it. I might raise that a bit if you had some other stuff to sell."

"Not at the moment. Maybe later. I'll keep this for now" – retrieving the ornament.

Mrs. Wingfield entered the yard. Sam said, "Okay, I'll give you a look when you've had more time for a sort out. Bye-bye for now." He gave her an amorous wink, nodded to Mrs. Wingfield, and departed.

"Imelda, it was very sweet of you to send me those two things for my collection," said Mrs. Wingfield warmly. "Have you found some additions to yours? – Some nice buttonhooks?"

"Yes, several. Come in, and I'll show you."

Although keenly interested in the contents of the house, Mrs. Wingfield did not stay long. "I don't want to delay you, my dear. I hope you were comfortable in your digs last night."

"Yes, very, thank you." Imelda told her briefly about Mrs. Walsham and her loneliness.

"Poor woman, I must see what I can do for her. These private housing estates which are mushrooming everywhere are terrible places for loneliness. All the people on them have been uprooted from somewhere else. May I come to the funeral on Saturday? I used to know Miss Partridge quite well, years ago, before she became a recluse. So it wouldn't be an act of hypocrisy on my part, and it might be less melancholy for you."

"Thank you. I wish you would come."

A number of people saw Miss Partridge's remains interred among the daffodils and leaning lichened gravestones in St. Benet's churchyard. Mrs. Medlar came with another woman and, to Imelda's surprise and discomfiture, Charles accompanied Mrs. Wingfield. But when he greeted Imelda, there was nothing in his expression to remind her of their last encounter. To give him his due, she thought he was present in case the service reminded his grandmother of other more painful funerals. The same thought had occurred to Imelda, and had made her regret accepting Mrs. Wingfield's suggestion. She knew the funeral would have distressed Mrs. Walsham, and for that reason had not mentioned it to her.

"Would you care to have lunch with us? – Or are you too busy?" asked Mrs. Wingfield afterwards. She seemed as composed and cheerful as ever.

"It's kind of you, but I have so little time left . . ."

Mrs. Wingfield did not press her. "Yes, I understand. Which train are you catching tomorrow?"

Imelda told her.

Sensing Charles's eyes upon her, she glanced up at him, and met a look which said clearly that, now, he was remembering the sugared-pill of her parting shot. To her vexation, she felt herself blushing.

"Shall we see you again in these parts?" he asked.

"I don't know. Probably not." She turned to Mrs. Wingfield. "So I'd better say goodbye, and thank you for everything."

The bones of Mrs. Wingfield's hand felt brittle, the flesh soft. But Charles's hand, which he offered and she could not ignore, was warm and supple. He did not crush her hand with painful force as large men were apt to do, but his clasp was firm, and she sensed the latent strength in his long brown fingers. Like Sam Mutford, she noticed, he did not smoke or wear rings, and she felt a flash of amusement at his probable reaction if he knew he was being compared with someone like Sam.

She spent the evening watching television with Mrs. Walsham who had agreed to take care of certain objects which Imelda did not want to leave in the house. Sergeant Saxtead had promised to keep his eye on the premises, but with any empty property there was always a risk of things being stolen.

If only I could make up my mind, she thought, staring with unseeing eyes at the television screen, while beside her on the settee Mrs. Walsham enjoyed the Saturday film.

Imelda had been spared the necessity of passing sentence on the cats. Mrs. Medlar was willing to adopt them, along with the budgerigars, if Imelda could afford a small remittance towards the cost of their food. She had agreed with relief. Sentimental as Charles might think her, she had scruples about the destruction of healthy animals as well as about abandoning them.

The following afternoon she was waiting for the bus to Norwich when a car slowed and pulled into the layby marked BUS STOP ONLY. From his place at the wheel, Charles Wingfield leaned across to thrust open the near-side door. "I'm going your way. Hop in."

As she seated herself beside him, she said with constrained politeness, "What takes you to the city on a Sunday?"

"You do, Miss Calthorpe. I knew you would have to use the two o'clock bus to catch your train, and I wanted to talk to you."

CHAPTER II

"WHAT about?" Imelda asked warily.

"First, about that 'mutual antipathy' you mentioned the other afternoon. My grandmother has taken me to task for being an unconvivial host during your short stay with us. The fact is that the night you arrived I had had a difficult day and was feeling thoroughly anti-social. It doesn't excuse my bad temper, but I hope it will convince you that although *your* antipathy may be justified, it is certainly not reciprocated."

She had wondered what he would be like when he set himself to be disarming, and now she was finding out. As he sat there, half turned towards her, his forearm resting on the back of his seat, she was sharply aware of his magnetism.

"I admit it must have seemed foolish to come rushing down here without finding out first where I could stay," she answered.

"Had I known that you had come straight from your mother's wedding, I should have admired your readiness to cope with the contingency instead of criticising you for lack of foresight."

The arrival of the bus made him straighten, and set the car in motion. As he checked that it was safe to pull out, he said, "What is your impression of Norfolk? Does it strike you as too flat and featureless?"

"Oh, no! I think it's a lovely county – at least, what little I've seen of it. I like being able to see for miles, and it isn't completely flat, is it? The country round here is quite undulating," she said, looking out of the window

41

at the passing scene. "I shall find London rather claustrophobic after all this openness."

Had she made the journey by bus, she would have had to change from the county to the city service to reach Thorpe Station. Consequently, in Charles's large car, she arrived there with forty minutes to spare. Instead of leaving her to fill this extra time as best she could, he put the car in the station's parking enclosure, and suggested they had coffee in the buffet.

Presently, passing the bookstall on the way to her platform, he bought her a *Sunday Times* and *Punch* to read on the train.

When she realised that he meant to buy a platform ticket, she said, "You've been very kind, Mr. Wingfield, but please don't feel you must wait till the train comes in."

"I'd almost forgotten that I have a proposition to put to you," he said, as he put a coin in the ticket machine.

"A proposition?"

Charles glanced at his watch. "Yes, and there are only ten minutes left in which to explain it. Beatrix Otley rang up this morning from some unpronounceable place in Wales. She drove over there on Friday in pursuit of a special piece of furniture for an important customer. I understand that on Thursday she came to see you at Miss Partridge's house – your house, as it is now."

Imelda nodded.

"The lease of her present shop in Norwich has only a few months to run," he continued. "The overheads are high, and for some time she has been hoping to find a suitable shop in the country. She has asked me to make you an offer of five thousand for your house."

Before she could say anything he went on, "I presume you won't take steps to sell the property before your mother returns from her honeymoon and you can discuss the

42

matter with her? You know, I expect, that estate agents charge a percentage of the purchase price, so that if one can find a buyer without recourse to an agent it's all to the good?"

"Yes, I do, but —"

"Also, Beatrix is willing to take the place as it stands," Charles continued. "There would have to be the customary legal searches, of course, but she says she's prepared to complete the clearing out which you've started. The contents were never of high quality and have been badly neglected, I gather."

"They don't compare with *your* furniture, and they have been neglected," said Imelda. "But I wouldn't describe them as worthless."

"But worth very little, according to Beatrix."

"Mrs. Otley doesn't handle Victoriana, and judging by her talk with me on Thursday she knows next to nothing about it," Imelda said dryly.

"You don't think her offer is a fair one? Perhaps you don't realise that property values in East Anglia are very much lower than in London. Another point to consider is that it isn't easy for people to get mortgages on old houses, and the type of people who can afford to pay for a house outright are unlikely to be looking for a place as small as yours. Its position, bang on the main road, is not in its favour," said Charles.

"Not for buyers in search of private houses," agreed Imelda. "But for a shop — which is why Mrs. Otley wants it — being on a main road is an advantage. Whether her offer is a fair one or not, I don't know. The question doesn't arise. I've decided to keep the house."

He lifted an eyebrow. "In order to let it, do you mean?"

"No, to live in it myself. Now that I'm no longer

43

needed at home, I've decided to try my luck as a dealer in curios and bygones."

Charles looked momentarily dumbfounded, and Imelda herself was taken aback by the resolute tone in which she had announced a decision which, an hour before, had not been made.

"My good child, you must be mad!" said Charles impatiently. "To contemplate opening a ... a wool shop would be most unwise. What you suggest is pure folly."

It was then that it dawned on her that for the past hour he had been making a fool of her. Everything he had said, beginning with his apology for not being nicer to her at the Hall, had been skilful soft soap to make her receptive to Mrs. Otley's offer.

It was easy to imagine him telling Beatrix, during their telephone talk, *I'm not an ideal intermediary. The girl doesn't like me.* And Beatrix replying, with a laugh, *You can soon alter that, Charles. Turn on the charm for a bit before you mention my offer. I'm sure you can make her succumb to you.*

And I did, thought Imelda, much mortified. I was beginning to think I'd misjudged him.

Aloud, she said, "It's not a suggestion, Mr. Wingfield. It's a carefully considered decision."

"Do you know anything about antiques?"

"I'm not going to deal in antiques in the purist's sense of the word. Mrs. Otley will call my shop a junk shop."

"There's a world of difference between browsing in junk shops for amusement, and making a living as a dealer."

"Obviously; but dealers are self-trained, not born. Anyway I don't see why you should be so concerned, apart from not wishing to fail Mrs. Otley," said Imelda.

His expression changed from one of impatient disapproval to a different kind of displeasure. He said coldly,

44

"What do you mean by that remark?"

Her reply was lost in the noise of the London train's arrival. When it came to a standstill, Charles stepped forward to open the nearest door for her.

"That's First. I'm travelling Second," she said.

He accompanied her along the platform to where a number of people were queueing to enter the corridor of a Second Class coach. On the fringe of the group, Imelda turned to him. "Goodbye. Thank you for the lift."

For a moment she thought he was going to persist in his arguments until the last moment. But to her relief, he said only, "I hope your family will be able to convince you of the unwisdom of your scheme." He took out his wallet, withdrew a card, and scribbled something on it. As he handed it to her, he said, "Those are Mrs. Otley's telephone numbers at the Lodge, and at her shop, should you wish to discuss her offer with her. Goodbye, Miss Calthorpe."

Imelda watched him stride down the platform until her view of his tall, straight figure was blocked by a motorised trolley piled high with cartons. Then she entered the train and found a seat.

Before she put Charles's card away in her bag, she looked at his name and address which were engraved on the face of the card. What had he *thought* she might have meant by her last reference to Mrs. Otley? she wondered. And why had it made him angry?

The next day, at the office, she gave a month's notice. But she said nothing of her plans to John and Lucy. That night she wrote to her mother and Ben, describing her visit to Norfolk, and also to Mrs. Walsham, to ask if the widow would be willing to have her as a lodger for the time it would take to make Miss Partridge's house habit-

45

able. Her third letter was to Sebastian Ellough, now resident in a private nursing home in Sussex.

For two years, following the death of his sister who had kept house for him, old Mr. Ellough had lodged with the Calthorpes. He had been a dealer in curios all his life, and it was he who had kindled Imelda's interest in old things. His personal passion was for the colour-printed lids which, in Victoria's reign, had helped to sell pots of pomade, fish-paste, cold cream and other commodities. He had owned a fine collection of Pratt ware pot-lids, and he had taught Imelda to distinguish between these and modern reproductions. Although pot-lids had never exerted their magic on her, she knew enough about them to recognise the two she had found in her great-aunt's house as rare specimens which, sold to a specialist dealer, would more than cover the cost of installing a bathroom and modern kitchen in her future home.

Following a slight stroke, Mr. Ellough had sold his business and left London for a country house community of comfortably-off old people where, should his health decline further, he would have professional nursing. Imelda had missed him very much, and had surprised her mother by writing to him regularly, and receiving lengthy replies in Mr. Ellough's spidery handwriting.

"I can't think what you find to tell him, dear," her mother had often remarked, unaware that, by virtue of a box full of buttonhooks, Imelda had joined the widespread freemasonry of collectors who could always find plenty to say to each other, however disparate their ages, incomes and other circumstances.

By return of post, she had a letter from Sebastian Ellough in which he wrote – "To my mind, the greatest tragedy in life is never to have the opportunity, or the courage, to follow one's bent. You have been an excellent daughter while your mother needed you, and now you have the chance to fulfil a dream which, a short time ago, seemed impossible. Take it, my dear, and good luck to you. Pay no attention to the doubting Thomases . . ."

The night the Derehams came home from Devon, Imelda had a celebration supper waiting for them. John had spent the holiday redecorating the master bedroom as a surprise for them and with part of the proceeds from the pot-lids, Imelda had bought material which she knew her mother admired, and had made new bedroom curtains and a bedspread to match.

Although by now she was bursting to drop her bombshell, she managed to contain her impatience for twenty-four hours after their homecoming.

When, at last, she told them, they listened in astounded silence until Imelda concluded her announcement with – "I'm afraid you will think it very selfish of me to decide all this without consulting you, when the sale of the house would be an advantage to all of us. But if, at the end of a year, the shop is a flop, the house will still be saleable, and probably for a higher price that it would fetch at present."

Her mother and stepfather exchanged glances.

"I think it's a splendid scheme, Melly," said Mrs. Dereham. "I've felt for some time that you weren't getting as much fun out of life as a girl of your age should, and Ben and I were hoping that now you would feel free to try for a job abroad, or something more exciting than your present one. We don't want you to leave home. We shall miss you very much. But it can't be many more years before you meet the man you want to marry, so now is the time to spread your wings."

"Even if, like Icarus, you wind up in the sea or, in this case, the bankruptcy court," said John, with a grin.

Imelda had been living in Norfolk for three days when, coming out of the Post Office, she met Charles Wingfield. She was sticking stamps on letters to London and Sussex, and they almost collided on the threshold. As he stood aside with a murmured apology, his mobile left eyebrow shot up, and he registered her workman's overalls worn over a threadbare pink shirt.

"Miss Calthorpe! So you meant what you said."

Considering that she did not like him, and had hoped to avoid an encounter with him for some time, Imelda knew it was irrational to be piqued by the fact that his recognition had not been instantaneous, as hers had.

"Good morning, Mr. Wingfield. I always mean what I say. Don't you?"

"Yes, but I am past the age of biting off more than I can comfortably chew."

"How dull for you," said Imelda. "I hope I shall always be ready to accept a challenging opportunity." And she turned away to drop her letters through the mouth of the posting box.

But as she walked up the street to her house she thought, I should have made an effort to be pleasant. I can't be on good terms with Mrs. Wingfield, and bad ones with him. I need friends here, not enemies – and especially not an influential enemy like Charles Wingfield. He is probably on the local council, and could make life awkward for me, if he chose.

Her first task at the house had been to tear down the filthy lace curtains which were obscuring more than half the light. Now the windows were washed and whitewashed which made the rooms much brighter, but preserved their privacy from the eyes of inquisitive passers-by.

Since it would be weeks, if not months, before she could live in the house, Imelda had decided to make one room presentable, and to start trading from it immediately. The room she had chosen was the parlour, not the original shop across the hall which was fitted with a counter and shelves. These might come in useful later, but for the present they were merely obstacles to the type of display she had in mind. According to old Mrs. Medlar, it was seven or eight years since anyone had bought anything from Miss Partridge, and Imelda had not yet had time to go through all the dusty boxes of haberdashery.

On the afternoon following her brief exchange with Charles Wingfield, she was on top of a step-ladder, painting the parlour ceiling, when from the back of the house came a shout – "Anyone about?"

Flexing her aching right arm, she went to answer the call and found Sam Mutford.

"Hello," he said. "How are you?"

Imelda was pleased to see him. He was her first contact with "the trade" in the locality, and she knew he could give her some useful tips about other dealers, particularly about the local "ring".

"I'm fine. How are you? Come inside. I'm just about to have my coffee break. Would you like a cup?" She led the way back to the parlour.

She had two vacuum flasks to keep her supplied with hot drinks, and the cup on the second flask was unused. She gave it to Sam, and filled the cup from the morning flask for herself.

"How's business?" she asked.

"Up and down. Made up your mind what you want to sell yet?"

"As a matter of fact I'm setting up in business myself. If you come round next week, this room will be full of things for sale, and I shall be ready to buy from *you*," she told him.

He drank some coffee, and gave her a speculative look. "Are you on your own?"

"Not entirely. I'll have someone to mind the shop when I'm out buying."

"Have you been in the trade somewhere else?"

"Not as the boss," she said, with a smile. It was an evasion of the question, but she did not want him to spread the word that she was a novice.

Sam said, "I've some stuff on the van which might suit you if you'd like to come outside and have a look."

He had several things which she liked including two framed prints of Victorian oil paintings, *The Awakening Conscience* and *Broken Vows*.

"But I haven't enough cash on me," she said, when they had agreed a price. "I wasn't expecting to do any buying yet."

"That's okay. You can have them on tick until my next call." He carried the pictures indoors for her.

Some rolls of Art Nouveau wallpaper which Imelda had chosen in Norwich the day before were on the table in the passage. Noticing them, Sam said, "I'm a pretty good paper-hanger. Do you want me to come round one or two evenings and put that up for you?" When she hesitated, he added, "Just to help you get straight a bit quicker. I wouldn't charge you."

"It's very kind of you, Sam. I'd be glad of your help. But there isn't any electricity yet."

"That's no problem. I know where I can borrow a portable generator."

Again Imelda hesitated. Sam said shrewdly, "If you're worried about being alone with me here after dark, you needn't be. You can ask Diane at the hairdresser's if you want to check. She used to be my girl until her mother decided a dealer wasn't good enough for her daughter, and

50

nagged Di to break it off. Di's not independent like you. Her mother could make her do anything."

"What makes you think I'm independent?"

"You must be to leave home and start a business on your own. If Di had to sleep in this old place, she'd be scared silly."

"So would I, in its present state," admitted Imelda. "It won't be so creepy when it's decorated, and there's electricity and a telephone. For the time being, I'm living in digs. If you're sure you can spare the time, Sam, I'd be glad of some help."

He was not certain that he could borrow the generator immediately, but, if he could, he would fetch Imelda from Mrs. Walsham's house at half past seven that evening, and he would start papering the parlour while she did the ceiling in the hall.

A short time after his departure she had a visit from Mrs. Wingfield.

"How are you, my dear? Charles told me he met you this morning, and I came to give you this." She opened her bag and took out something wrapped in tissue paper.

It was a buttonhook with a handle of ivory inlaid with the pinpoints of gold known as *pique d'or*.

"It was with a jumble of things, all very dirty, in a lacquer workbox which I bought at an auction some time ago," explained Mrs. Wingfield. "I cleaned it, and put it away, and forgot about it until a few days after your return to London. If you hadn't come back, I meant to ask Sergeant Saxtead for your address, and post it to you. Now you're back, I want you to have it as a small 'good luck' present."

Imelda was delighted. The hook was a rare one, and by far the most beautiful she had seen. She thanked Mrs. Wingfield warmly. "Do *you* think I'm crazy to open a junk shop?" she asked.

"As a matter of fact, I envy you. It's what I've always wanted to do myself," said Mrs. Wingfield. "I agree with Beatrix that Victorian furniture is not to be compared with the lovely furniture of the eighteenth century, and the Regency. But I have a weakness for the bits and pieces of Victoriana which Beatrix regards as rubbish. Things like scrapwork screens, and sand pictures, and shell bouquets in glass domes. After my husband died, and I moved to the Lodge, and had less to do, I did toy with the idea of opening a shop myself. But Piers and Rowena were horrified, so I gave it up. Piers was always rather a stickler for the done thing, unlike Charles, who has never given a hoot for public or family opinion as long as *his* principles are satisfied. Had you known them both, you would never have taken them for brothers."

"I can see that the children aren't like him, at least not in looks," said Imelda.

"Ah, the children take after their mother," explained Mrs. Wingfield. "Rowena was a lovely blonde creature. She was a stickler, too, but I don't think she was inherently super-conventional. It was the result of her upbringing. Her father is a retired General, and a more stuffy old warhorse I have yet to meet. He runs his family like a regiment. When Rowena married Piers who, in some ways, was very like her father, her girlhood and married life merged with no break in the pattern. Had she chosen Charles, who knew her first, she might have developed quite differently."

Her glance fell on *Broken Vows*, propped against the wall. "Now *that* appeals to me very much. I like all the Pre-Raphaelite artists, but my favourite Victorian painter is Tissot. If you should ever come across a Tissot print, I wish you would put it aside for me."

Walking to Mrs. Walsham's bungalow for the evening

meal which would be waiting for her, Imelda found herself puzzling over Mrs. Wingfield's reference to the difference in character of her two grandsons.

Imelda's impression of Charles was that he fitted his present position perfectly. When she had met him that morning, in his old but once expensive country clothes, with the labrador loping behind him, he had looked every inch a landowner. To hear him called unconventional did not accord with her picture of him, although it tallied with Sergeant Saxtead's description – "a bit of a rolling stone".

The only disadvantage of lodging with Mrs. Walsham was that the meals she provided, although delicious, were extremely fattening. Imelda hoped that the exercise involved in putting the house to rights would counteract the calories in Mrs. Walsham's home made meat pies and feather-light steamed puddings. Her landlady was one of those people who refused to accept the connection between food and fatness, and Imelda was reluctant to hurt her feelings by not eating heartily. But she had been a plump adolescent, and was loath to risk her present slenderness.

About a quarter past seven, as Imelda was helping Mrs. Walsham to do the dishes, Sam's battered blue van drew up outside.

Imelda introduced him to Mrs. Walsham, who eyed his hair, and his brigand's moustache, with ill-concealed disapproval.

"Your landlady is a bit like Di's mum," said Sam, as they set off for the house. "Spends half her life worrying whether her neighbour's got a bigger and better telly, I shouldn't wonder."

"Oh, I don't think Mrs. Walsham is too bothered about keeping up with the Joneses," said Imelda mildly.

"Di's mum is. 'What will the neighbours say?' is her thought for the day – every day!" Sam said scathingly.

Imelda glanced at his scowling profile. "Has Di found another boy-friend now?"

"Yes, some weed in the Income Tax Office," he said, with a snort.

During the evening, Imelda asked him what other antique shops there were in the area, and mentioned that she had already met one of the city dealers, Mrs. Otley.

"Oh, her." He grinned reminiscently. "I don't often come across anything good enough for her. She's at the top end of the trade. She's also the kind of person who thinks someone like me must be dead ignorant. She was talking to me once, and she said, 'I have a customer who collects white china discs with children's names on them in blue, and sometimes a date. If you can find any for me, I'll give you two pounds each for them.'" He finished pasting a length of paper. "Do you know what she was talking about?"

"Lowestoft birth plaques?"

"That's right. I don't know exactly what they're worth, but I know it's a ruddy sight more than two quid. My mother is pally with a woman up the street who cleans for Mrs. Otley. The gossip is that Mrs. O. is hoping to move from the Lodge to the Hall before long. There's no Mr. Otley, you see, and the bloke at the Hall is a bachelor, and she fancies her chances there. Maybe you've met him yourself. Now I come to think of it, old Mrs. Wingfield came round here the same day that I did."

Imelda explained her acquaintance with Mrs. Wingfield. "It was she who introduced me to Mrs. Otley. What happened to Mr. Otley?"

"Haven't a clue. Maybe he died, maybe they didn't get on. I –"

54

A rap at the front door interrupted him.

"Oh, Sergeant Saxtead – good evening. Come in," said Imelda, when she saw who was outside.

"I saw the light and thought I'd check it was someone who ought to be in here," said the Sergeant, following her into the parlour.

"Do you know Mr. Mutford who's helping me to re-decorate?"

"Yes, we've met," said the Sergeant, nodding to Sam.

Imelda said, "I've been meaning to call at the Police Station to thank you again for putting me in touch with Mrs. Walsham. I'm staying with her until this place is organised. I'm opening a shop called Victoriana."

The Sergeant did not stay long, and when he had gone neither Beatrix or Charles came into the conversation again.

"How about a quick drink at the Unicorn before I run you home?" suggested Sam, when they had finished work for the night.

Imelda was longing for a hot bath to ease her aching arm and shoulder, but she felt she owed it to Sam to be sociable.

"Yes, but only on condition that you'll let me buy you a drink as a token 'thank you' for your help."

"Listen," said Sam, rather curtly, "I wasn't hinting for free beer. I don't agree with all this Women's Lib. stuff. If you're so independent that you want to go Dutch, let's forget the whole idea."

"Okay, you pay for the drinks," said Imelda mildly. She wondered if it was only his pride which had been stung by the break with Diane, or if the injury went deeper.

The last bus back from the city was setting down passengers as Sam and Imelda crossed the road to the Unicorn. The lounge bar was not very crowded. Several people greeted Sam, and looked with curiosity at Imelda.

Sam introduced her to the landlord, who said, "Very pleased to meet you, miss. We've been wondering what was going to happen to old Miss Partridge's place. It being over a month since she passed away, and no Sale board going up, it was a bit of a puzzle to us. So you're opening an antique shop, eh?"

Sam didn't ask what she would like to drink. Perhaps he was astute enough to guess that she was not a beer-drinking girl, and she wouldn't ask for a short drink. He said, "You've been on your feet for a long time. Have a brandy and soda . . . a pint of keg bitter for me, George."

Presently some more customers came in, and George moved away to attend to them.

"You know what you ought to do, Imelda," said Sam, "You ought to put a Wanted card in the Post Office window. It would only cost sixpence a week, and it might bring in some good stuff."

She was asking him if there was driving instructor in the area, when the door of the bar opened again and a very pretty fair girl came in. At the sight of Sam, who was leaning on the bar, facing the door, while Imelda perched on a stool, the girl hesitated, causing the young man behind her to bump against her.

"Oh . . . hello, Sam," she said, in a soft voice, her face turning pink.

"Hello, Di. Hello, Melvyn." Sam's manner remained equable. Had he not said the girl's name, Imelda would have thought their connection was no closer than that of former classmates.

Melvyn's reaction, however, was markedly hostile. He uttered a brusque "Evening," and hurried Diane to a vacant table on the other side of the room.

It would not have surprised Imelda if Sam had begun to put on a show of heavy flirting with her. But he continued their conversation without any change of manner, thereby reinforcing her opinion that he was a much more intelligent and subtle person than his appearance might suggest to a casual observer.

"I'll teach you to drive, if you like," he said to her, on the way home.

"Thanks, Sam, but I'd rather take lessons from a professional instructor, if you don't mind. I want to take a crash course. But I expect I'll be glad of your advice when it comes to buying a second-hand car."

"I'm glad you're back, dear," said Mrs. Walsham, switching off the television as Imelda entered the sitting-room. "I was worried about you being alone in that old house with that young man."

"Sam isn't dangerous," Imelda said, smiling.

Mrs. Walsham bustled to the kitchen to make cocoa. She was wearing a quilted dressing gown, and a ruched net cap over rollers and pin curls. Imelda thought how uncomfortable it must be to sleep in all that headgear. Her mother wore her hair in a bun and when she unpinned it at night, and it fell about her shoulders, she looked oddly girlish. Thinking of her family in London, she felt a twinge of homesickness.

"Well, perhaps not, dear," said Mrs. Walsham, her mind still on Sam. "But I can't say I like these long-haired young men, and that long moustache looks horrible, if you ask me."

"His hair is very clean." It was no use arguing about hair with people of Mrs. Walsham's generation, thought Imelda. But it seemed to her that, shorn of his Viking locks, Sam's face would be indistinguishable from the good-humoured, tough, reliable faces of the British sol-

57

diers whom Mrs. Walsham had been watching admiringly on the television screen a few minutes earlier.

On the second Sunday after her return to Norfolk, Imelda and Mrs. Walsham had lunch at the Hall. Imelda had accepted the invitation partly because she knew it would thrill Mrs. Walsham, and partly because she had found several things in the house which she wanted to show to Mrs. Wingfield, and to discuss with her.

Mrs. Wingfield picked them up in her car on her way home from church. While she was talking about the Women's Institute to Mrs. Walsham, Imelda sat behind, feasting her eyes on the countryside which, just now, was at the peak of spring perfection, and trying to ignore the butterfly-flutterings inside her at the prospect of another ordeal-by-Charles.

Perhaps he would not be at home today. But if he were, he would not be likely to discompose her in the presence of his grandmother and another guest, she reflected.

Upon their arrival at the Hall, it seemed that he would not be present at the lunch table. The children appeared, their hair brushed, their hands very clean, and were introduced to Mrs. Walsham. The grown-ups sipped sherry and chatted. And then at the very last moment, after Mr. Betts had come to say, "Luncheon is served, madam," and they were on their way to the dining-room, Charles came hurrying downstairs, apologising for his lateness.

His arrival flustered Mrs. Walsham who had just been starting to relax. Not for the first time, Imelda saw Charles exerting himself to be agreeable. His technique was equally successful with Mrs. Walsham, she observed.

Turning to his grandmother, she said, "I've fallen in love with a bracelet which I found at the bottom of a buttonbox, but I'm not at all sure what it's made of, and I

58

wondered if you might know. It's jet black, and very light in weight, but it isn't as glossy as jet."

"It sounds to me like *bois durci*, which was the very earliest plastic. It was invented by a Frenchman, and made from ebony dust and albumen," said Mrs. Wingfield. "Did you bring the bracelet with you?"

"Yes, and one or two other small things which puzzle me. After lunch I'll show you, if I may?"

But when lunch was over, Mrs. Wingfield seemed to have forgotten the bracelet, as she said, "Charles always takes the children for a ramble on Sunday afternoon. Why don't you join them, Imelda? Mrs. Walsham and I will stroll leisurely round the garden."

"When does Victoriana open?" asked Charles, as they set off across the park.

"Oh, you've noticed my new signboard," she said, pleased at this unexpected proof that the blue and gold board was as eye-catching as she had hoped. "The parlour will be open tomorrow. I'm not sure when the shop – the original shop – will be ready. Probably not for some weeks yet."

"I'm surprised you're opening so soon, even in a limited way. You must have worked very hard."

Imelda was about to say that she could not have managed without Sam's help, when Sophie asked her, "May we come to see your shop when we spend our pocket money on Saturday?"

"If your grandmother has no objection – certainly."

"Mrs. Otley doesn't allow children or dogs in her shop in case they break something."

"The things in Mrs. Otley's shop are more valuable than my stock. I was once in an antique shop with another customer who had a very well-behaved dog. It sat quietly all the time its owner was looking round. Everything was

59

fine until the very last minute, and then something terrible happened."

"What?" asked Sophie, round-eyed.

"As they were leaving, the dog started to wag its tail. Before anyone could save them, two lovely pieces of porcelain were brushed off the top of a low table."

"What happened then?"

"The dog's owner had to pay for the damage."

"How much? A hundred pounds?"

"No, anything as valuable as that is usually kept in a cabinet. Possibly ten or twenty pounds. I don't know exactly."

By now they were following a cart track which led to a five-barred gate at the edge of some woodland. The gate was padlocked, but this was no obstacle to the children who swarmed up the bars while Poppy pushed through the hedge.

"Can you manage this in a skirt?" asked Charles, as he and Imelda arrived at the gate.

"I expect so." She mounted the bars, wishing she had on a trouser suit.

He swung over the gate with the practised ease of a long-legged countryman, and Imelda, had she been unobserved, could have managed the matter without much difficulty. But somehow Charles's presence made her nervous and consequently awkward. Concerned not to snag her tights, and wishing the man would walk on, instead of waiting and watching, she clambered inexpertly over, then poised to jump to the ground. As she balanced there, Charles stepped forward and grasped her waist and lifted her down.

Imelda had not reached twenty without quite often being in the posture in which she was now. Usually, when a man held her by the waist and looked into her eyes, his next action was to kiss her. In varying degrees she had enjoyed these experiences, without ever being swept off her feet. In her view, being swept off one's feet was something which happened rather rarely, and then only to emotional, dreamy girls, not to down-to-earth ones like herself.

So it was unnerving to find that, although Charles had no thought of kissing her, the thought of being kissed was in her own mind, with an effect which could hardly have been more disturbing had he actually done it. In the instant before he released her, and they resumed their walk, her heart began to thump. Her legs felt weak. Her mouth felt dry.

As he let her go, the children came running back to them, and she had time to pull herself together, and to start being annoyed with herself for responding to a man's physical magnetism when, by all the important criteria, she did not like him.

The object of the walk was to gather primroses in a part of the wood where they grew in particular abundance. Presently, while Henry and Sophie were climbing a tree, and Imelda was picking flowers and listening to Fanny, they heard hoofbeats coming along a ride which led to the glade from another direction.

"Here comes Mrs. Otley," said Fanny.

Imelda glanced towards Charles. He was lounging in the sun, with his back against the trunk of a beech tree. He seemed to be lost in thought, perhaps half asleep, and it was only when horse and rider came into view that he bestirred himself.

"What a glorious afternoon!" remarked Beatrix, in her high, clear voice, as she brought her mount to a halt in the centre of the clearing.

"Yes," said Charles, strolling forward to stroke, with an accustomed hand, the animal's velvety nostrils.

61

To Imelda, who knew nothing about horses, it looked a large and rather highly-strung animal, but probably Beatrix had been riding all her life. She looked wholly at ease, and very attractive in her cream breeches and amber jersey. Her hair was almost the same glossy chestnut as the horse's coat.

She dismounted, and Sophie and Henry slithered down from their tree, and ran up to pat the horse.

"I don't like horses," Fanny confided to Imelda. "They're too big. I like guinea-pigs better."

"Haven't you a pony?" asked Imelda. Had she given the matter any thought, she would have assumed that all the Wingfields rode, and were only refraining from riding this afternoon because they had guests who did not ride.

"No," said Fanny. "We have stables, and two funny old carriages which were used instead of cars when Granny was little. But we haven't any horses now."

Beatrix, after speaking to the older children, looked round to see where Fanny was, and caught sight of Imelda.

"Oh . . . Miss Calthorpe. Good afternoon. I hear in the village that your shop will be opening tomorrow."

"Good afternoon. Yes, it will."

"Well, I wish you luck with your venture, and hope you won't regret it," said Beatrix. "If ever you have anything brought in which you think might be genuinely antique, you're welcome to ask my advice."

"Thank you," Imelda said meekly. She wondered if Mrs. Otley meant to be patronising, or if it was unintentional.

"Charles, the Forncetts are coming in for drinks this evening. They're bringing a cousin of Barbara's who's spending the weekend with them. He sounds one of those fascinating characters who's been everywhere and done everything. Would you care to join us, and to meet him?"

"I'm afraid I can't tonight, Beatrix. I have to go out."

"Oh, what a pity." If she was more than mildly disappointed she did not allow it to show. There was nothing in her manner to support the gossip, spread by her daily help, that she had a matrimonial interest in Charles.

Changing the subject, she said, "I do wish you would let me teach this child to ride. She's aching to learn, aren't you, Sophie?"

The little girl nodded. "All the girls in my form ride. Couldn't I? *Please*, Uncle Charles?"

He shook his head. "No," he said quietly but with finality.

"Come on, Sophie." Henry tugged impatiently at her sweater.

"Why are you so against riding?" said Beatrix, when they had run off to their tree. "It's not only a healthy activity, but it teaches children so many valuable moral lessons."

"It can also teach them to be thoroughly objectionable little pot-hunters," said Charles dryly.

"Yes, sometimes it does, I admit – but not invariably. It isn't necessary to go in for gymkhanas and show-jumping."

"Even without that side of it, it's still an expensive pastime, Beatrix."

She smiled. "Are you pleading poverty? Oh, Charles! A pony for Sophie would cost much less to run than your car. However, I won't argue with you, if you're really opposed to the idea. Perhaps you think riding makes girls less feminine?" she added, with a touch of coquetry.

It seemed to Imelda that his mouth had tightened a little at the reference to his car. But perhaps she was mistaken, for he answered, "It would be difficult to hold that view in the face of such striking evidence to the contrary," and Beatrix smiled and looked pleased.

A few minutes later she mounted and rode away, calling to the children that she would see them at eight-fifteen the following morning.

"Mrs. Otley takes us to school in her car because she has to go to Norwich anyway," Fanny explained to Imelda. "In the afternoon, Uncle Charles and Granny take turns to fetch us. Henry comes home by himself on the bus, later than we do."

Returning to the house by a way which avoided the high locked gate, they found Mrs. Wingfield and her other guest sitting on a sheltered seat against the mellow brick wall which enclosed the stable yard.

Imelda felt it was time to leave, and with unflattering alacrity Charles said he would run them home, and went off to get out his car.

Presently, sitting behind Mrs. Walsham, a position from which all she could see of his face was his temple and cheekbone, she wondered if it were possible that the Wingfields were no longer as rich as they had once been, and that Charles kept a rein on other expenses in order to indulge his own sybaritic tastes, of which the car was an example.

"*That* will give them something to talk about," remarked Mrs. Walsham to Imelda, as the car slid away from her gate, watched by most of her neighbours who, on fine Sunday afternoons, mowed the grass in the front gardens and washed and polished their own cars.

Imelda smiled at her landlady's satisfaction at giving the neighbours cause for conjecture for a change. Charles had been punctilious in escorting his passengers to their front door, but he had not accepted Mrs. Walsham's invitation to come in and have a cup of tea.

"I had such a nice chat with her while you were out walking with him," Mrs. Walsham went on. "*Her* life hasn't been what you might call a bed of roses, in spite of them being moneyed people, and having that big house and everything. She was telling me that her husband was lamed in the First War, and when they lost both their boys in the last lot, it just about finished him, poor man. Funny the grandson isn't married, specially now he's responsible for the three kiddies. Some women in her position wouldn't want him to marry, of course. But from what she told me, she'd prefer to give way to a younger woman. You'd never dream she was seventy-four, to look at her. I wouldn't have put her at seventy."

"Mrs. Wingfield is a darling," said Imelda.

"He seems a nice young chap, too – well, young to me, but not to you, I suppose. I'd put him somewhere near thirty. There'll be plenty of girls around here on the catch for him, I expect," said her landlady, with a knowing chuckle.

"Possibly."

Mrs. Walsham gave her a shrewd glance. "Don't you like him?"

"He's attractive. I can't say I've noticed anything else in his favour. He hasn't his grandmother's qualities."

Imelda was too excited to sleep well that night, and at half past six on Monday morning she crept out of bed and went to the kitchen to make herself a cup of coffee. As she waited for the kettle to boil, she wondered if Charles Wingfield had been right when, on the station platform five weeks ago, he had described her plan to open an antique shop, without any previous experience, as "Pure folly".

Shivering slightly, in spite of being snugly clad in a blue and white quilted dressing-gown which her stepfather had given her last Christmas, she thought: What if my customers are mainly browsers, with hardly any trade buyers? What if I can't replace my existing stock? What if I make some appalling mistake, like paying far too much for something worthless, or selling something valuable too cheaply?

For a while she was stricken with misgivings. But soon after seven the post brought a letter from London, wishing her luck, and a flat package from Sussex. In it she found a silver-handled magnifying glass, and a note from Sebastian Ellough in which he said he had used the glass throughout his own career as a dealer, and wished her to have it as a useful memento of their friendship.

Imelda was delighted with this unexpected present, and before she dressed she wrote a letter of thanks to post on her way to the shop. Her confidence had returned and, at a quarter past eight, she set out from the bungalow. There were one or two finishing touches which she wanted to make before opening for business at nine.

It was a fine morning with the promise of a hot noonday, and to attract attention to the fact that Victoriana was ready for customers, she put a small table on the pavement outside her front door, and on it placed various oddments and shabby books, all for sale at tenpence or less.

The parlour was furnished in much the same way as she had found it, but with everything cleaned and polished, and with fresh white paint replacing the dirty varnish on the woodwork. None of the three parlour pictures had been of much interest, but Imelda had made use of the frames which she had washed and brightened with gilding wax. Now, one of the frames surrounded a remnant of padded red silk to which she had fastened several brooches, a Victorian campaign medal, a pair of jet mourning ear-rings, and a number of interesting buttons and Edwardian hatpins. With the help of Sam, the two other frames had been converted into doors for shallow display cases. In these she had put fragile or valuable objects such as the child's china mug with a whistling-bird handle, found in the pantry, and a pair of ornate silver sugar nips discovered, black with tarnish, at the back of a drawer in the deal-topped table in the scullery.

At nine-fifteen, after a number of passers-by had peered through her shining clean window, the old-fashioned doorbell began to jangle, and Imelda entered the hall from the kitchen and smiled a welcome at her first customer.

By the end of the day she had made the acquaintance of three established dealers from other parts of the county, she had made friends with two private collectors – a farmer who collected desk seals, and a housewife in search of lace bobbins – and she had watched with concealed amusement while a number of local people who had nothing better to do that morning had come in to see the house which for so long had been a mystery to them.

At five, Mrs. Wingfield called, and Imelda was able to confide that not only had her sales been satisfactory, but two people had come in with curios they wished to sell to her.

Taking Mrs. Wingfield to the kitchen, she said, "I bought these spelter figures from an old lady who says she has some other things she doesn't want, and a man brought in this stuffed owl."

"Which I will buy for Henry's birthday – if it's not too expensive," said Mrs. Wingfield. "Three things he has wanted for ages are an ostrich's egg, a boomerang, and a barn owl."

"He is rather an endearing bird. I was hoping he would
67

stay with me for a while," said Imelda, when the sale was settled.

"I will leave it here for tonight, if I may? I'll smuggle it home some time tomorrow. Henry's birthday isn't until next month. Before I pay for the owl, let me see what else you have to tempt me."

Presently, in the parlour, she said, "Your prices seem very fair, Imelda. I thought perhaps, coming from London, you might be inclined to overcharge."

"I hope not. What concerns me is that I have practically nothing which a child could afford to buy."

"Yes, that's one of my problems. Both Henry and Sophie are keen to start collecting, but everything which appeals to them is far too expensive for their pockets. Charles is the only member of the family who seems to lack the acquisitive urge. He buys a good many books, but they're his only self-indulgence. I think he regards possessions as an encumbrance. Even his cottage in Menorca, where he was living when Piers was killed, has only the essential furniture."

"He has a beautiful car."

"Oh, that isn't his car, my dear. It was Piers who was mad about cars. Charles decided to keep it because, although it is heavy on petrol, it won't depreciate as rapidly as my little runabout."

When, at half past five, Imelda was about to lock up, Sam Mutford drew up in his van.

"How did it go?" he enquired, as she crossed the pavement in response to his beckoning gesture.

"Splendidly! Better than I hoped. Have you had a good day."

"Not bad. Can I interest you in a good set of fire-irons for a fiver?"

She bought the fire-irons, a brass letter rack, and a biscuit tin in the shape of a book. As she counted notes into Sam's palm, he said, "There's a good film on in the city this week. We could have some Chinese nosh afterwards. Do you good to have a night out."

"I'd like to, Sam, but I'd have to give Mrs. Walsham more than an hour's notice. She goes to a lot of trouble with my evening meals. I couldn't dash in and announce that I wouldn't be there to eat whatever it is she's prepared for tonight."

"Okay – how about Friday?"

Imelda hesitated. Without Sam's help, Victoriana would not have been ready to open for some time yet, and apart from being grateful she liked him. Nevertheless she had an intuitive feeling that it might be wiser to keep their friendship within certain bounds, at least for the time being.

Sensing her uncertainty, Sam said, "Maybe you're already booked. Some other time perhaps. See you . . ."

As he turned away, she said impulsively, "Friday would be fine, Sam. Will you pick me up from my digs? What time should I be ready?"

After he had driven away in the opposite direction, Imelda walked home, wondering if she had been foolish to accept his invitation chiefly because he had looked so hurt when he thought she meant to refuse.

Although Wednesday was early closing day throughout the county, Imelda decided to keep the shop open all week until experience showed which was the most suitable half-day for Victoriana. Remembering that Thursday was the slackest day at Mrs. Otley's shop in the city, she was not surprised when, on Thursday afternoon, she had a visit from Beatrix.

"How are you getting on so far?" was her first remark.

"Fairly well," Imelda said cautiously.

Beatrix looked round the parlour, but made no comment on the transformation since her previous visit. "Business usually is quite brisk for the first week or two. Then it tends to tail off." She picked up an unmarked but good quality Parian figure. "Oh . . . damaged!" she said, with a slight grimace.

"That's why it's so cheap," said Imelda. "Some collectors don't mind slight damage if the price is reduced accordingly. Do you stock only perfect pieces, Mrs. Otley?"

"The porcelain I sell is worth expert restoration when it's been damaged. The cost of repairing this would be more than its value as a perfect piece, I should imagine." Beatrix replaced the figure, and turned her attention to a fruit dish of purple carnival glass. "This is collected in America, I'm told."

"Yes, although I agree with you that it's hard to see why," said Imelda, saving Mrs. Oxley the trouble of saying something disdainful about the dish.

Beatrix flickered a glance at her. Presently, after looking at several other objects, she startled Imelda by buying a trinket box made of porcupine quills. It seemed an odd choice in view of her expressed contempt for the more attractive examples of Victorian taste.

"What will you do with yourself in the evening, once you've finished putting the place in order?" she asked, while Imelda was wrapping the box. "Apart from some evening classes at the Secondary Modern School, and such things as bingo and whist, there's very little to do here Won't you find it dull after London?"

"Life isn't a continuous whirl of gaiety in our suburb," Imelda said dryly.

"But you did have your family behind you, and you made contacts at work, I expect."

"Not as many as I hope to make as a dealer."

"I meant social contacts," said Beatrix.

"So did I. Surely a strong mutual interest is the best kind of social contact? Don't you find that some of your customers gradually become friends as well?"

"Occasionally," Beatrix agreed. "But I wouldn't have thought that many young men were interested in ... er ... curios, and at your age it's natural to want plenty of boy-friends."

Imelda fastened the parcel with sticky tape. "Would you like a receipt, Mrs. Otley?"

Beatrix shook her head, and looked in her bag for some money. "Have the Wingfields been down to see you since Sunday?"

"Mrs. Wingfield has."

"As she is a collector, I expect you will see her from time to time. The Wingfields are very kind in the way they try to make welcome any newcomers they hear of. They were charming to me when I arrived. But one has to remember that they do have their own private circle of people with the same background, the same interests ..."

At this point another customer came in, and Beatrix paid for the box and left.

On Friday, leaving Mrs. Walsham in charge of the shop for half an hour, Imelda went to a jumble sale where she bought two pots of home-made jam for her future store cupboard, a potted plant, several books, and a pair of ivory glove-stretchers with carved handles.

When she returned to the shop, she was surprised to find Mrs. Walsham in conversation with Charles Wingfield.

"I'll be off, dear, now that you're back. Did you buy anything nice at the sale?"

"There were no unrecognised treasures. Don't rush away, Mrs. Walsham."

"I mustn't stop. I've some shopping to do. See you later, dear."

As her landlady left, the doorbell jangling in her wake, Imelda began to unpack her basket. Among the books she had bought was an early edition of *Little Lord Fauntleroy* which she thought might appeal to the schoolmistress who had followed Beatrix into the shop yesterday, and whose interest lay in old-fashioned books for children.

"Did you buy this at the jumble sale?" asked Charles, picking up the new-looking copy of *Bayard* by D. G. Hepburn which she had just placed on the table.

"Yes, but it's not for sale, I'm afraid. I bought it to keep for myself. Are you a Hepburn fan, too?"

"I have all his books."

"Two guineas was too expensive for me. I had to wait for the paperback. I couldn't believe my luck when I spotted that copy for twenty-five pence. Can you understand anyone giving it to a jumble sale? Perhaps the person who owned it has died."

"Possibly." Charles put the volume on the table. "My grandmother bought a stuffed owl from you for Henry's birthday."

"Yes . . . is there something the matter with it?"

"I haven't seen the bird yet. She has it secreted somewhere. What I came to ask is if you would keep an eye open for a suitable present for her own birthday in July."

"Certainly," said Imelda. "I've already promised her an option on any needlework tools which pass through my hands, and if anything special turns up – a really fine

72

workbox, for example – I can let you see it before she does. The only snag is that nothing good in her line may come in between now and July."

He nodded. "I realise that. But if it's possible, the children and I should like to give her something more personal than chocolates or gloves, or any of the commonplace presents."

For the second time in their acquaintance, Imelda felt herself thawing towards him. "I'm hoping to go to some auctions, when I'm more settled. I might spot something at a sale. What sort of price had you in mind?" Before he could answer, she added quickly, "I wouldn't take advantage of knowing how much you are willing to spend."

A quizzical gleam lit his eyes. "On the contrary, I think you're more likely to do yourself down. It was the obvious softness of your nature which made me doubt your fitness to open this shop."

"And do you still doubt it?" she asked.

"I think you're more knowledgeable about your wares than I'd realised. Whether you're a competent judge of people is another matter."

"Well, as long as I recognise a treasure or a fake when I see it, I can't be duped by a phoney person," she said lightly.

"Not as a dealer. As a girl you might be," said Charles. "What is this little gadget?" He had picked up a small silver object which, with a silver hunter and a muff chain, had been lying on the black plush pad of a wooden collecting plate.

"That's a napkin-holder. The hooked end fixes through a waistcoat buttonhole, and the discs grip the edge of the napkin and prevent it from slipping to the floor."

He cocked an eyebrow. "You really do know your stuff."

"I know a little. I still have a great deal to learn."

"Who did your decorating? You haven't done all this yourself?" – with a gesture at the wallpaper and paintwork.

"No, I've been very lucky. A man who lives here has helped me. He's in the trade too, but as a runner."

"What does that involve?"

"He has no premises. He buys from the trade, or at sales, and sells to the trade. We met when he called to see if I wanted the house cleared."

"A useful contact in several ways," Charles remarked. "You say he's a local chap. What's his name?"

"Sam . . . Sam Mutford. Do you know him?"

To her surprise, for she had expected him to shrug and shake his head, the mention of Sam's name caused Charle's dark brows to contract in a frown of disapproval.

When he said nothing, she asked, "Why do you look like that?"

The doorbell jangled. A woman in a camel trouser suit came in. "May I have a look round?"

"Please do." Imelda's smile was somewhat distraite.

As Charles walked into the hall, she followed him. "Why don't you like him?" she asked, in a lowered voice.

He looked down at her perplexed face, his own expression enigmatic. "The last time I gave you advice, it wasn't too well received. This time I'll only say that if you value your reputation you won't encourage a connection with someone who is about as disreputable as they come." He glanced over her head at the woman hovering in the parlour. "I think your customer needs you. Goodnight, Imelda."

CHAPTER III

CHARLES'S admonition, added to her own reservations about becoming too friendly with Sam, caused Imelda to dress for the evening in a mood of considerable uneasiness. Had Mrs. Walsham possessed a telephone, she would have been tempted to ring up Charles and press him to be specific about his grounds for warning her against Sam.

Had he meant that Sam was dishonest? Surely, if that were the case, Sergeant Saxtead would have put her on her guard?

Perhaps Charles disapproved of Sam for much the same reasons that Diane's mother had against him, thought Imelda, as she reached into the wardrobe for the dress she was going to wear.

She was ready before Sam arrived.

"I hope that young man doesn't drink too much," remarked Mrs. Walsham. She had been animadverting in this fashion ever since Imelda had announced her date.

"I shouldn't think so. If he lost his driving licence, he would lose his living."

Her landlady sniffed. "It seems a queer sort of living to me. Can't he find himself a proper job? – Or doesn't he want to?"

"That sounds like him now," said Imelda, hearing a motor slowing down. "Goodnight, Mrs. Walsham. I'll do my best not to disturb you when I come in. Don't worry: I shan't be too late."

As she opened the front door, Sam was crossing the

pavement outside the gate. The vehicle parked at the kerb was not his shabby old van, but a smart blue saloon.

"I've borrowed my brother's car. It's more comfortable than the van," he explained, smiling at her.

Seeing how he was dressed, Imelda wished she had waited for him to ring the bell. Sam in a suit, with a patterned shirt and plain tie, looked very different from Sam in jeans and a leather jacket. She would have liked Mrs. Walsham to see him. But although it was not quite dusk, her landlady had already drawn the curtains. The moment a light was switched on in the bungalows, the picture windows so beloved by estate builders gave the sitting-rooms as little privacy as goldfish bowls.

"We shall have to get a move on. The second film starts at seven-thirty. How are your driving lessons going?" he asked, as he set the car in motion.

"Pretty well, I think. But I've no experience of city driving yet. I'm still chugging round country lanes, practising gear changes."

They arrived at the cinema in Norwich with seven minutes to spare before the last performance started. Sam had driven fast, but never recklessly. He bought two Front Circle tickets, and a box of chocolates from the kiosk.

The film had attracted a large audience, and the house lights were on as they edged their way along a row towards two vacant seats in the centre.

Murmuring, "Excuse me ... thank you," to the people who had risen to let them pass, Imelda found herself wondering if, by an unlucky chance, Charles had also chosen tonight to see the film.

Why would it be unlucky? she asked herself, as she sat down. Why should I mind if Charles did see me out with Sam?

Although, once the main feature had started, the boy in the seat in front of her spent most of the film nuzzling his girl's ear, to Imelda's relief Sam's arms remained folded across his chest, and his attention concentrated on the screen.

Only when the programme was over, and the audience streamed out of the building, did he take her hand to steer her through the crowd to the car park.

In the car, they discussed the film, and were still talking about it when Sam pushed open the door of the restaurant. It was not until the Chinese waiter had taken their order for honey barbecued spare ribs to be followed by sweet and sour prawn balls, and had hurried away to fetch lager for Sam and ginger beer for Imelda, that it seemed the right moment for her to delve in her bag and produce a small, neatly wrapped package.

"I know you would be offended if I attempted to pay you for everything you've done at the shop," she began, "so this is a very small present in appreciation of your kindness."

He opened the package in silence, and Imelda wondered nervously if a nineteenth-century cravat pin made of a small cabochon garnet set in gold was a wildly unsuitable present. She had found it in a *papier-mâché* box in a drawer in the best bedroom, and concluded that it had belonged to Miss Florence's father, Isaiah Partridge.

"You didn't have to give me anything," said Sam, rather gruffly. He stuck the pin in his tie. Looking down at his chest, he said, "I've always fancied one of these. It looks great. Thanks, Imelda."

Seeing that his pleasure was genuine, she relaxed. "By the way, Sam, have you seen any boot-scrapers lately? A woman came in today who's looking for one. She bought the cast iron brolly stand, and the curtain poles with the

77

wooden rings, and I think she may become a regular."

"I have seen a scraper somewhere. Can't remember where," he said thoughtfully.

They began to talk shop.

This was a pleasure which Imelda had experienced only with Sebastian Ellough, and then in a somewhat different form because Sebastian had known so much more than she did. With Sam she was on an equal footing. In some fields, she was the wiser; in others, he was.

Watching him as he dealt with the bill, she realised he was the first young man with whom she had ever had something in common. With all the others there had been nothing but a mutual attraction, which was enough to launch a relationship, but not enough to sustain it for more than a month or two.

Several times, in the past, she had thought how pleasant it would be to meet someone who was like Sebastian, but forty years younger. There were young men in the antique trade, but the only ones she had encountered had been patently uninterested in girls. There was nothing effeminate about Sam. He was as masculine as ... as Charles Wingfield.

Thinking of Charles – twice in one evening! – made her frown. How aggravating it was to be attracted to a man whom she disliked, and not attracted to Sam who, in all ways, she liked immensely.

"What's the matter?" he asked, noticing her expression.

Imelda smiled at him. "Nothing. It's been the nicest evening I've had for ages, Sam."

Perhaps she infused a little too much warmth into her tone, for, when they had left the restaurant, again he held her hand on the way to where the car was parked; and there, for an apprehensive moment, she thought he was going to kiss her. Perhaps he changed his mind, or perhaps the thought had not been in his mind, only in hers. To her relief, he released her and unlocked the car, and soon they were on the road home.

For a mile or two Sam was silent, which seemed to confirm her intuition. Oh, lord – I hope he isn't planning to follow their example, she thought, as the headlamps scanned a layby and lit up a parked car with two people in it.

Although by now she had made a good many bus journeys to the city and back, it was the first time she had noticed the large number of laybys on the way. Each time they approached one, she could not help tensing a little in case Sam should ease his foot off the accelerator and flick on the nearside winker.

"I know where it was I saw that scraper!" he exclaimed suddenly. "It was out at the back of old Oulton's place. Next time I'm over that way, I'll see if he'll take fifty pence for it. He's a cross-grained old devil sometimes, but – What's the joke?" – glancing at Imelda, and seeing that she was smiling to herself.

"No joke. Just a passing thought. Is old Oulton a dealer?" she enquired.

He shook his head. "He's a pensioner now. Used to be a coachman in his young days. Still wears those thick leather gaiters."

He was talking about the old countryman, and the strange assortment of bygones to be found in the sheds behind his cottage, when they reached Mrs. Walsham's darkened bungalow.

"Not exactly night owls, your neighbours," Sam remarked, noticing the absence of any lights other than street lamps and the dipped beam of the car's headlights.

"No, and we mustn't disturb them or there may be complaints to Mrs. Walsham about *my* late hours," said

79

Imelda, undoing the lock on her safety belt.

Sam stretched his left arm along the back of her seat, but only to pull up the safety catch on the door. "You'll be more of a free agent when you're in your own place. Can you cook?"

"Well, I'm no Margaret Costa, but I can knock up a reasonable meal."

"Right: you can cook one for me. Roast pork with plenty of crackling, and apple pie."

"I'll make a note of it. Goodnight, Sam – and thanks again for a super evening." She opened the door and climbed out on to the pavement. Although it was not yet midnight, the noise as she closed the door behind her seemed very loud in the silence which shrouded the estate.

She had no sooner opened the front door than the light went on in Mrs. Walsham's bedroom. The door was half open. Her landlady's voice called nervously, "Is that you, Imelda?"

"Did I wake you? I'm sorry. I was as quiet as I could be," said Imelda, putting her head round the door.

Mrs. Walsham was sitting up, and reaching for her bed-jacket.

"Yes, you were very quiet, but I wasn't asleep. Would you like a cup of tea? I made a flask before I came to bed. I knew I shouldn't be able to settle until you were safely back, dear."

"You make it sound as if I'd been on a dangerous mission," Imelda said, smiling. She wanted to take off her make-up and go to bed, not to sip tea and submit to a cross-examination. But she knew she was lucky to have found such comfortable temporary lodgings, and if some unnecessary fussing was part of the price, she must bear it with a good grace.

It was a quarter of an hour later before, on the pretext

of tiredness, she was able to escape to her own room. Actually she was not sleepy, and spent some time thinking over the evening, and admonishing herself for her conceit in assuming that because he had asked her out Sam must find her attractive. There were several possible motives for his invitation; the urge to show Diane she was not the only pebble on the beach, the impulse to be kind to a stranger, his own loneliness, combined with a wish to cement a useful business connection.

One morning the following week, Imelda left Mrs. Walsham in charge of the shop, and caught the bus to Norwich. There were a number of reference works which she could no longer do without, but before she ordered new copies – one of the books she needed cost more than ten pounds – she intended to try her luck at the second-hand and antiquarian bookshops. The yellow pages of the telephone directory had aided her in making a list of the city's bookdealers, for Sam never dabbled in books beyond checking that any old albums he came across did not incorporate musical boxes.

Towards midday, Imelda was carefully examining a fifteen-pound copy of *Queen Victoria's Dolls*, when a voice said, "Hello, what brings you here? It isn't often that one sees the female of the species in these surroundings."

She had heard the footsteps mounting the winding stairs to the upper room where she was browsing, and had thought they were made by the proprietor who had been up and down several times since her arrival. The last person she expected to see standing in the doorway was Charles Wingfield.

"Oh . . . isn't it?" she answered, responding to the statement rather than the question.

"Now I come to think about it, I don't believe I've ever

seen a woman in here. I suppose there are women biblio-philes, but they must do their book-hunting in catalogues rather than shops. What is your particular weakness?" — coming to stand behind her so that he could look down over her shoulder at the book she was holding.

"I'm not a proper book collector. I came in to see if they had an encyclopaedia of porcelain marks," she explained. "I was only looking at this book out of curiosity. What brings *you* here?"

It seemed to her that he hesitated. "The Brothers Grimm. I'm astonished to find that my nieces have never heard of Rapunzel or Snow White and Rose Red." He began to look along the shelves. "Perhaps you haven't either?" he added, with an interrogative glance at her.

"Yes, of course I have," she protested.

"The girl who teaches Sophie and Fanny is about your age, and she tells me that fairy tales are out of date. In her expert opinion, modern children want modern stories," said Charles sardonically. "However, while I'm doing the reading, I'll decide what is suitable and what isn't."

"Do you read to them much?" asked Imelda, rather surprised.

"To the girls — yes. Not to Henry. My grandmother can't be expected to cope with every aspect of their welfare. As it is, she has much less leisure than she ought to have at her age. Speaking of leisure, do I gather that you're having a day off?"

"Oh, no, only the morning. Mrs. Walsham is holding the fort for me." She glanced at her watch. "I must fly."

"To the bus station?"

"Yes."

"No need. I'll run you back."

Imelda hesitated. "It's very kind of you, but I promised to be back by one o'clock."

82

"So did I. Aunt Boadicea is coming to lunch, and she's a stickler for punctuality. If I'm not at attention on the doorstep when she arrives, there'll be the devil to pay. I'm in her black books as it is."

"Boadicea?" she echoed. Could Mrs. Wingfield have named her daughter after the warrior-queen of the Iceni?

He grinned. "My aunt was christened Margaret, but Boadicea is far more appropriate, as you'll see if she calls at your shop on the way home. She lives in Suffolk, and she's coming over to discuss the arrangements for the children's summer holiday."

At the foot of the stairs, on their way out of the shop, they encountered the proprietor, who said, "Good morning, Mr. Wingfield. I didn't know you'd come in. What a fortunate coincidence! I should have telephoned you later. I've had a report of *Letter From a Gentleman at Mahon*."

Charles introduced him to Imelda, and for some minutes the two men discussed the book the proprietor had mentioned. It was evident from the bookseller's manner that Charles was a regular and valued customer. Imelda remembered Mrs. Wingfield saying that he bought a good many books, but she had not implied that her grandson was a serious and erudite collector. Yet this was the impression Imelda was receiving now as she stood quietly at his elbow, listening to a conversation sprinkled with terms which she recognised, without understanding them, as the special jargon of the antiquarian book trade.

"What sort of books do you collect?" she asked, as they walked round the corner to where he had left his car.

He gave her a guarded glance. "Having a cottage in Menorca has given me an interest in the history of the island. It was held by the British for the greater part of the eighteenth century, and I've picked up one or two books about that period."

83

His tone was casual to the point of being off-hand. But Imelda had the feeling that he was deliberately making light of a matter of deep importance to him.

When they were seated in the car, before he switched on the engine, Charles looked at her again. He said, "You have lost what my grandmother calls 'the London look'. The first time you came to Norfolk, you were too pale – and too thin. Do you feel better for living in the country for a time?"

"I don't know that I feel any healthier. I feel much happier," she conceded. "It's wonderful to be a square peg in a square hole after years of being stuck in a round hole."

A curiously sombre expression came over his face. "Yes," he said abruptly. "Yes, that's the most important thing in life." And he switched on the motor, and gave all his attention to the business of edging out of a tight parking space.

They were only a mile from the city when there was a loud bang, and the car ahead of them suddenly slewed on to the grass verge and jolted to a standstill.

"Tyre's gone," said Charles succinctly, braking and steering his own vehicle on to the grass.

Imelda followed him back to where a middle-aged woman was emerging, visibly shaken, from a small grey saloon. "Oh . . . Mr. Wingfield," she murmured, recognising him. "Oh, dear – what a nasty sensation!"

"You handled it splendidly, Mrs. Runton. Don't worry: I'll soon change the wheel for you. Go and sit in my car with Miss Calthorpe."

Within ten minutes the spare wheel had replaced the burst tyre, and Charles was kindly but firmly insisting that the still upset Mrs. Runton should resume her journey home.

"It will probably never happen to you again," he assured her. "But anyway we'll be right behind you."

Half a mile further on, he cocked an amused eyebrow at her cautious thirty-mile-an-hour progress, and said to Imelda, "You'll just about make your deadline, but I shall definitely be too late to salute Aunt Boadicea."

His tolerance in keeping the big car at a comparative crawl, and tucked close to the nearside verge so that it did not impede the passage of any following traffic, was another revelation to Imelda. She would have expected him to have little patience with women drivers who could not take a burst tyre in their stride.

"Why are you in your aunt's black books?" she asked.

A crease appeared in the lean cheek nearest to her. "She disapproves of my interests," he said enigmatically.

"Why should she call at the shop? Does she collect?"

"If she didn't, one would suspect that the nursing home gave my grandmother the wrong infant. Apart from Aunt Margaret's mania for treen, they're completely unalike. Which is why I'm not sure it's a sound idea for them to share Na Vell for a month this summer."

"Na Vell?"

"My house on the island. Hasn't Grandmother mentioned the plan to you?"

Imelda shook her head.

"My aunt's son and his wife are in Japan for a year, and she has charge of their child," he went on. "The idea is that, as I can't be away for six weeks, Aunt Margaret should use this car to drive a combined party to Spain, returning by air at the end of August when I would fly down for a short break before bringing them back. Four children in the back is rather a squeeze, but at least my aunt could cope with any contingencies of the sort Mrs. Runton has just experienced" – with a nod at the car in front of them. "Grandmother is amazingly energetic for her age, but I'm not happy about her making the journey on her own, which is what she intended before my aunt put up her plan."

"How far is it?" asked Imelda.

"Roughly nine hundred miles from Calais to Barcelona where they catch the boat to Menorca. Most of the island's summer visitors get there by air, of course. But in the circumstances, neither Grandmother or the children are too keen on flying."

"No, naturally not," she said gravely. "But you spoke of flying there yourself."

Charles shrugged. "The chance of another member of the family being involved in an air crash is negligible." A pause. "The accident didn't have the same emotional impact on me as on the others."

Glancing at him, she saw the frown which had accompanied the last remark. But even as she looked at him it cleared and, obviously wishing to change the subject, he said, "I gather you've had no joy with regard to finding a birthday present?"

"Not yet, I'm afraid."

A few minutes later he dropped her outside the shop.

It was shortly before closing time when his aunt called at Victoriana. She was a tall woman with gingery colouring and a no-nonsense manner. Although she did not look more than fifty, she had none of her mother's charm. Even in her seventies, Mrs. Wingfield was an attractive person, still capable of inspiring affection and probably offers of marriage. But Margaret Letheringham − as she introduced herself − had the look of a woman who, given the choice, would have preferred to be a man. Her clothes were good and serviceable, but lacked any sense of style. Her hair was the standardised result of a weekly visit by an unexacting customer to a mediocre hairdresser. Her hands were those of someone who does not bother with rubber gloves, cream or nail polish. How such a woman could have grown up under Mrs. Wingfield's aegis, it was hard to understand.

"My mother tells me that you're rather more knowledgeable than many of the people who call themselves antique dealers nowadays," remarked Mrs. Letheringham briskly. "I assume therefore that I need not explain to you what treen is?"

"Would 'useful objects made of wood' be a satisfactory definition?" asked Imelda. "But I haven't much to offer you," she added. "This smoker's compendium, and the saltbox and the pocket spice-grater are all I have at the moment."

Her customer inspected the grate critically, and decided to have it – "less the usual ten per cent, of course."

"You're not in the trade, are you?" Imelda asked politely.

Mrs. Letheringham snorted. "Certainly not! But my mother says you always give her a discount."

"Mrs. Wingfield is one of my best private customers."

"I daresay I shall buy from you quite frequently – if you have suitable pieces to offer me, and if you stay open."

"I hope so. But I'm afraid I can't reduce the price of the grater," said Imelda, who thought it bad form to haggle the first time one bought at a shop. She had never done so as a collector, and was antagonised by it now that she was a dealer.

"Oh, come now, surely as Charles' aunt I rate some preferential treatment," said Mrs. Letheringham, becoming jovial. "You certainly enjoy his esteem. He speaks very favourably of you, which is more than can be said of several extremely nice girls to whom I've introduced him. No doubt you share his taste for books and history, and all that sort of thing."

"I'm interested in them — yes. But my acquaintance with your nephew is very slight."

"Really? That's not the impression I had formed from what he told me."

At this point, someone else came into the shop, and evidently Mrs. Letheringham did not care to press the matter of a discount in the presence of another customer. She said, rather irritably, that she would take the grater.

When she had gone, and while the other customer was browsing through a box of old sepia *carte de visite* photographs, Imelda wondered if Charles had talked about her, or if that was merely a ploy by which Mrs. Letheringham had hoped to gain her discount.

The shop was empty, and she was about to lock up, when the telephone rang.

"Elizabeth Wingfield here. Has my daughter been to see you?"

"Yes, she has. She bought a spice-grater."

"And haggled furiously about the price, no doubt," said Mrs. Wingfield, with a chuckle. "Margaret is an incurable bargain-hunter. I rang up to ask if you would care to come to a dinner party we're having at the end of next week, Imelda? Most of the guests will be a good deal older than you are, but I think you might enjoy it nevertheless."

"I should love to come, Mrs. Wingfield. How very kind of you to ask me. Which day next week, and what time?"

Mrs. Wingfield told her, and added that she need not worry about how to get to the Hall as Charles would fetch her and take her home.

Walking home for supper, Imelda realised that she had forgotten to ask Charles what he meant when he had said that Sam was "about as disreputable as they come." But the thought of Sam flitted only briefly through her mind. Her chief preoccupation was what to wear to dine at the Hall. She had never been to a large private dinner party before, and there was nothing in her wardrobe appropriate to such an occasion. Nor was there time to make a dress. Her only recourse seemed to go to Norwich and buy one, assuming she could find something she liked and could afford. An enthusiastic home-dressmaker, she grudged spending money on mass-produced garments when, for half the price, she could produce a more meticulously finished "original". What she would have liked to wear at the dinner party was an Edwardian skirt of stiff silk, a wide velvet belt, and a blouse with leg-o'-mutton sleeves. But to make such a combination in ten days, without the aid of her mother's sewing machine, was an impossibility.

She was pondering the problem afresh at the shop the next day when a middle-aged woman with a suitcase came in, and said doubtfully, "I don't suppose you buy clothes, do you? Old clothes, I mean?"

"It depends how old," said Imelda. "You'd better come through to the back room. There's more space there."

The woman introduced herself as Mrs. Hockwold, the chairman of a church working party in a village a few miles away.

"We've just held a jumble sale to raise money to buy the canvas and wools for a special set of kneelers," she explained as she snapped open the suitcase. "These clothes were a contribution which, unfortunately, no one wanted to buy. Then suddenly I thought that perhaps you might be interested. There are one or two moth holes here and there, but everything is perfectly clean."

Most of the garments in the case were relics of the 'Twenties and 'Thirties, but at the very bottom was a black silk bodice and skirt of a much earlier period.

As soon as Mrs. Hockwold had departed with her now empty suitcase, Imelda wondered if it had been madness to buy the Victorian dress to wear at the Wingfields' dinner party. Supposing it had been given to the jumble sale by one of the other guests? She did not even know if it would fit her. It might have been made for a girl with a seventeen-inch waist.

On Monday morning, Imelda went to Norwich to take her driving test. In the afternoon she had her first solo drive in the second-hand car which, on Sam's advice, she had bought from a retired schoolmistress whose failing eyesight had forced her to sell it after less than a year of careful use. In the evening, Imelda wrote a note to Mrs. Wingfield in which she explained that it would not be necessary to put Charles to the trouble of fetching her. At the back of her mind, she hoped that he would telephone the shop and insist upon fetching her.

The day before the dinner party, she arrived at the shop to find a letter from her mother on the mat, and another envelope addressed in a shaky handwriting which she did not recognise. The letter inside was written on a leaf torn from a notebook. It was signed Rosanna Titchwell (Mrs.), and it said that the writer had some articles for sale if Imelda cared to call and see them.

During the morning, Mrs. Walsham looked in on her way home from the butcher's shop, and she agreed to take charge for an hour while Imelda called on Mrs. Titchwell.

The old lady lived at one end of a row of red brick, slate-roofed cottages. Even to Imelda's London-bred eyes, it was obvious that the front door and brocatellecurtained "front room" were seldom used, if at all. She made her way round to the back of the building.

A faint voice from within answered her knock on a door at right angles to a window through which, a few moments later, she glimpsed someone beckoning to her. Opening the door, she passed through an old-fashioned scullery into the room where, although it was a warm, sunny morning, Mrs. Titchwell was sitting close to a small coal fire.

The objects the old lady wanted to sell filled a cardboard carton. As she went through them, Imelda's heart sank, for most of the contents were either of little interest to her, or damaged.

"How much do you want for these things, Mrs. Titchwell?" she asked, looking through the 1892 edition of Mrs. Molesworth's *Robin Redbreast* which would have been worth buying had it not been so badly damp-stained.

"Oh, I've no idea what they're worth. You'll have to tell me that, my dear. But my home help says all these old things are worth quite a bit of money nowadays. There's a programme she sees on the television. I forget what she said it was called, but I expect you know the one. Mrs. Harpley is always talking about it, and that's what gave me the idea of selling some of my old things. Will you have a cup of tea, dear?" – tapping the vacuum flask on the table by her chair. "My neighbour brings it in twice a day. They've stopped me keeping a kettle on the fire. They think I may have an accident."

Imelda sipped a cup of the dark, sweet tea, and chatted, inwardly torn between her wish to offer the old lady several much-needed pounds, and her knowledge that the things in the carton were not worth more than a few pence.

"You haven't any old sewing tools? Pincushions, needle-cases, that sort of thing?" she enquired.

"I don't think so. You can look in the basket, if you

like. It's in the cupboard over there. I haven't used it for a long time," said Mrs. Titchwell.

The basket contained a tangle of darning wool, old suspenders, a much-mended grey lisle stocking and a crêpe bandage mixed up with cards of linen buttons and black hooks and eyes. At first, when Imelda spotted the walnut, she thought it must be an ordinary one. Then she saw the tiny hinge and knew that, incredibly, she had come upon a real treasure. With fingers suddenly unsteady, she opened the walnut. One half of the shell was hollow, lined with rose-coloured silk. The other half was covered with a piece of gilt metal in which were slots and sockets containing a tiny pair of scissors, a miniature bodkin, an embroidery stiletto, a thimble and a half-inch bottle of scent.

"What's that you've found, dear? Oh, the walnut. Do you know, I'd forgotten I had it. A pretty little toy, isn't it? They made things so nicely years ago."

"Where did you get it?" asked Imelda.

"It came to me with some things my sister left. My sister Ellen who died several years ago. I suppose it was given to her when she was in service. She worked for some very nice ladies, and they often gave her little presents."

"Would you sell it, Mrs. Titchwell?"

The old lady smiled. "If you like it, you can have it, my dear. If I'd remembered it was there, I'd have given it to Mrs. Harpley's granddaughter when she used to come to see me. But she's too old for such things now, and I don't know any other children."

Imelda held the nut in her palm. A fresh dilemma confronted her. She was almost certain that, about two years ago, she had read of a similar walnut fetching fifty pounds at an auction. But she was not certain; and even if she had been sure, she suspected that a handsome offer might be such a shock to the old lady that it could make her ill. It seemed wisest to make a generous offer for the other objects, and to add to the payment later on.

"I couldn't give you more than ten pounds, Mrs. Titchwell," she said, with a gesture at the carton of rubbish.

"Ten pounds! Good gracious me! I didn't expect more than two. To tell you the truth, I thought Mrs. Harpley was exaggerating," the old lady confided.

She was so flustered and excited by her good fortune that Imelda knew it would not have done to tell her the truth about the walnut. She would have to break the good news to her by degrees.

"You won't make a fortune out of that lot," Mrs. Walsham remarked tartly, when Imelda had returned to the shop, and was unloading the carton.

"No, but I didn't give much for it. Any customers?"

"Only a man wanting Tunbridge ware. I showed him the paper knife and the pencil box, but they didn't interest him. He was after the more unusual pieces."

Mrs. Walsham was becoming quite knowledgeable. The night before she had almost missed one of her favourite television programmes by becoming immersed in a book about Staffordshire portrait figures which Imelda had left in the sitting-room. Imelda foresaw the time when her landlady would fall in love with some antique object and want to own it. She was waiting with interest to find out what it would be. Probably something unexpected. People often succumbed to the most unlikely objects, rather in the same way that girls were attracted to unsuitable men, mused Imelda.

Like me and Charles.

The thought slipped into her mind, and was instantly dismissed, although she knew that not thinking about it wouldn't alter the fact. On the other hand, if she allowed thoughts of him to linger, it would worsen her condition which, at present, was only a very mild weakness.

During the afternoon, Sam stopped by with a loaded van. Imelda bought an Edison phonograph with six cylinder records, a pole screen, a box of lead soldiers, and a set of small mother-of-pearl dominoes in a shabby velvet bag.

While he was having a cup of coffee with her, she told him about the walnut and how she was torn between the wish to let Mrs. Wingfield have it at a bargain price, and the feeling that for Mrs. Titchwell's sake she ought to make as much as possible.

"You've forgotten something," said Sam.

"What's that?"

"Your cut. You'll never make a good living by buying high and selling low. Mrs. Wingfield's not short of a penny. If it's worth fifty quid, let her pay fifty. Although if you ask me anyone who'd pay all that for a walnut must be out of their minds. How old is it?"

"Not very old. About a hundred and thirty years, or thereabouts. But so few of them have survived. I've never seen one before. Anyway, I'm not positive that it's worth as much as that."

"If you've given the other old girl a tenner, and made her happy, I should hang on to it until you're in London and can sell it to one of the posh specialist dealers," advised Sam. He saw that she did not agree, and went on, "You can't mix sentiment with business. I don't hold with robbing anyone – specially not an old age pensioner – but you can't be too soft-hearted in this game."

"No, I suppose not. But sometimes I can't help feeling rather a parasite. I know Mrs. Wingfield would jump at this for twenty pounds" – turning the walnut between her fingertips – "but what have I done to deserve to make a ten-pound profit? Nothing at all."

"You knew what it was," Sam said firmly. "You knew because you've studied old things. Where would collectors like Mrs. Wingfield find what they want if there weren't any dealers? *She* wouldn't go poking about in old cottages, asking people if they had anything to sell in her line, and they wouldn't approach her off their own bat. Dealers are like any other shopkeepers, girl. They supply a demand. It's about time the small dealers did make a decent living. My old man can remember when nobody wanted to know about this sort of stuff" – waving his hand at the contents of the back parlour where they were sitting.

"Now it's going to the other extreme. Too many people are interested, and there aren't enough nice old things to go round," she said thoughtfully. "At least not at reasonable prices. I think you're right, Sam. Fifty pounds *is* a crazy price to pay for a walnut. On the other hand, think what thousands of engaged couples pay for a pathetic crumb of carbon which, but for the artificial scarcity created by the diamond corporations, would be no more expensive than a rhinestone."

On the afternoon of the dinner party, Imelda left Mrs. Walsham in charge of the shop, and crossed the road to the hairdressing salon. Her hair was shampooed by a junior, and she had to wait for a few minutes before Diane finished perming another customer and came to attend to her.

"Good afternoon. Sorry to keep you waiting. Did you just want a trim?" Diane's voice was soft, and perhaps a little affected.

"I'd like about two inches cut off, please." Imelda found it impossible to tell whether the younger girl recognised her as Sam's companion at the Unicorn.

Diane did not talk while she was cutting. She concentrated on what she was doing, and Imelda studied her pretty face, embellished with all the latest tricks of make-up, and wondered what she was like inside the beauty-queen exterior.

While the junior was sweeping up the wet ends of Imelda's hair, Diane placed a dry towel round her shoulders, and said, "You're the young lady from the new antique shop, aren't you?"

"That's right. And you're a friend of Sam Mutford, I believe?"

"I know him." The girl looked uneasy. "His sister was in my class at school. She's married now, and moved to Royston. If you live in a small place like this, you get to know most people, don't you?"

"I suppose you do," said Imelda. "It was fortunate for me that Sam was one of the first people I met here. He's helped me in all sorts of ways."

Diane was silent for some minutes. Then, lowering her voice so that it would not be audible to the girl seated at the reception desk – the two other customers were under the dryers – she said, "Yes, Sam is all right. It's the others who aren't very nice."

"The others?"

"The rest of his family. His mother and father, and his uncle." She paused, and then blurted, "His mother comes shopping in her slippers, with her hair in rollers. And his father has been had up in court for using bad language in a row with their neighbours. There's always some trouble with that family. My friend Jean was different, and Sam's brother Barry isn't a rough sort. But the rest of them – well, they're awful!" – with a grimace.

"'You choose your friends, Fate chooses your relations'," Imelda quoted dryly.

Diane looked momentarily blank. When she saw the

point, she said primly, "Yes, I daresay. But you don't have to live with them, do you? Not at his age." She studied Imelda's reflection in the mirror. "Don't you mind being away from your family?" she asked. "I shouldn't like being all on my own in a strange place."

Later, watching the girl from her seat under the dryer, Imelda thought her very pretty, but far too dim to be a fit wife for someone as shrewd and quick-witted as Sam. She would probably be obsessively house-proud and baby-proud, and totally uninterested in Sam's business.

Imelda had returned to Victoriana, and Mrs. Walsham had gone home, when Sam called.

"Your hair looks nice," he remarked. "Did Diane do it for you?"

"Yes, she did. Mrs. Wingfield has invited me to a dinner party tonight," she added, to explain why her hair was arranged in an Empress Eugénie chignon instead of tied back in a tail.

"I suppose she told you a long tale about me," he said, with an uncharacteristic scowl.

"On the contrary, I told her some things about you," Imelda answered lightly. "Were you . . . are you still keen on her, Sam?"

He studied the toes of his boots for a moment. "No," he said. "Not any more."

He raised his head and looked at her, his eyes very blue and bright with some strong emotion which Imelda hoped she misread and which caused her hurriedly to talk about something else.

There were already several motors on the sweep when Imelda arrived at the Hall that evening. Carefully, she parked her little car alongside a stately grey Bentley, and took a final glance at her make-up in the rear-view mirror. Then she climbed out and shook down her skirts.

Carefully pressed and repaired, the Victorian dress looked very different from the bundle of creased black silk which had failed to attract a buyer at Mrs. Hockwold's jumble sale. Imelda had not only filled two or three gaps in the row of sixteen jet buttons which fastened the bodice, she had stitched an edging of pleated white lawn inside the velvet cuffs and the high neckband.

The door was opened by Betts who, to her surprise, said, "Good evening, Miss Calthorpe." She had not expected him to remember her name.

As she entered the house, Mrs. Wingfield emerged from a room on the right of the hall. She was wearing a pink silk shirt with a long skirt of amethyst wool.

"Imelda, my dear, how are you? I was hoping to pop in at the shop this morning, but I was waylaid by someone and by the time I escaped it was too late to come and browse. It's been that sort of week. What delightful things have I missed?"

"None," Imelda assured her. "I've had two interesting thimbles, but I've put them aside for you to see."

"Nice child!" Mrs. Wingfield patted her arm, and led her into a large and beautiful drawing-room where, as a man finished speaking, a ripple of merriment ran round the group who had been listening to him.

"This is Imelda Calthorpe who owns the new antique shop in Church Street," said Mrs. Wingfield, taking advantage of the natural break in the conversation to present Imelda to everyone there. But as her hostess told her their names, Imelda's wits were temporarily numbed by her consciousness that they were all staring at her with expressions of astonished amusement. Two of the other women were wearing trouser suits in different shades of crushed velvet, a third was in a fine wool caftan, and Beatrix Otley

98

had on a long crêpe skirt, and a cowl-necked silk jersey top. Their casual expensive elegance made Imelda sinkingly aware that her own dress was ludicrously out of place.

She was neither young enough, or shy enough, to be overthrown for very long. But she was unnerved for several minutes, and therefore glad to be spared a decision about what to drink.

Instead of asking her what she would like, Charles brought her a glass of sherry, and stayed to listen to what an old man – whose name she had not registered – was telling her about the hardness of the local water.

Presently Mrs. Wingfield went away to welcome some more arrivals, and the old man remembered something he particularly wanted to say to someone across the room. Charles and Imelda were left alone.

"I wonder if, later on, there might be a chance to see you privately," she said quietly. As his eyebrow lifted, she went on, "I have something in my bag which I think your grandmother might like for her birthday. But perhaps you would rather come down to the shop to see it?"

His eyes glinted. "It isn't beyond my powers to arrange a tête-à-tête with you after dinner. I shall look forward to it."

She knew he was only teasing her, but nevertheless she felt a fluttering of the pulse.

At dinner Charles sat at one end of the table with a woman of Mrs. Wingfield's age on his right, and another elderly woman on his left. From her place near his grandmother's end of the table, Imelda avoided looking in his direction. The first time she did so, he was listening to a conversation between the women on either side of him, and Imelda had the impression that, in spite of his apparent attention to what they were discussing, his mind was on something else.

The second time she permitted herself to glance at him, she found he was looking at her. But whether consciously or absently she could not judge in the seconds before she averted her gaze.

After dinner, everyone returned to the drawing-room where, when nearly an hour had gone by, she thought he must have forgotten their private talk. Then suddenly he was at her elbow, waiting for a pause in her conversation with some other guests to extract her from the group and steer her to the library.

This was another room which she had not seen before tonight. The sight of the book-lined walls, the massive mahogany desk, and the Chippendale winged chairs on either side of the fire, made her give a murmur of pleasure.

Behind her, Charles closed the door. As she turned, intending to say, "What a marvellous room," he forestalled her.

"Alone at last," he said softly.

As before, he was only joking. But, as before, it made her throat tighten. What would it be like, she wondered, wth a shiver of excitement, to be really "alone at last" with a man like Charles? As the summer advanced, each time they met his face was browner. Tonight his tan was accentuated by the whiteness of his dress shirt, and beneath the sardonic black eyebrows the cold North Sea grey of his eyes was doubly unexpected.

But although the colour of his eyes might be incongruous in that otherwise dark southern face, there was nothing cold in their expression at the present moment. From whatever cause – and boredom seemed the most likely – he was in the mood to flirt with her, if she was willing.

"I – I'm afraid the thing I've brought for you to see is rather expensive," she said, opening the beadwork purse which she had taken out of stock for the evening. She handed the tissue-wrapped walnut to him.

He took it, but did not unwrap it immediately. "I like your dress. Is it the genuine article, or only a copy?"

"It's genuine. Can't you smell the mothballs?" she said lightly.

"Not from here. But perhaps if we were waltzing –"

Disconcertingly, he came close, slipping the walnut into the pocket of his dinner jacket in order to take her left hand in his, and rest his other hand on her waist. "No, even here I can only smell your scent. No mothballs . . . and no whalebones either, apparently" – sliding his hand further round her and drawing her closer. "Or have you removed them?"

"There were no bones to remove." Imelda disengaged her hand, and stepped backwards, away from him. "About the present for your grandmother. You must say if you don't care for it, or if the price is far too high. I can easily sell it elsewhere."

Charles' mouth curled with amusement. He took the package from his pocket and began to unwrap it, pausing to say, "You seem almost as nervous as the girl who first wore that dress would have been in this situation."

"What situation?"

"Being alone with a man."

"Not at all. I'm concerned not to keep you from your other guests longer than is necessary," she answered evenly.

Watching him, as he examined the walnut, she thought that although social customs changed with each generation, the essence of people's relationships did not alter very much. There must always have been men with whom the most timorous girls felt at ease, and other men, of whom Charles was one, in whose company even self-possessed girls could be thrown into old-fashioned flutters. Just why this should be so was hard to analyse.

"Expensive, you say?" Charles remarked.

"Thirty pounds."

As she expected, his eyebrows shot up. "Rather more than I had in mind."

"I know. But it's an exceptional item, and I thought you would want to see it before I showed it to Mrs. Wingfield."

"Do you think she will buy it if I don't?"

"I think so. I can't be certain, of course."

The door opened and Beatrix entered the room, stopping short when she saw it was occupied. "Oh ... I'm sorry. I didn't think anyone was here. I slipped away from the party to look up something in the encyclopaedia," she explained.

"Which volume do you need?" asked Charles, placing the walnut on the desk and turning towards the bookshelves.

"It isn't important. What's that?" – eyeing the walnut.

"A bibelot for Grandmother's birthday. Do you think it will please her?"

Beatrix picked up the walnut. Her hands were beautifully shaped, but spoiled, in Imelda's opinion, by long lacquered nails. Tonight she was wearing several rings. The diamonds sparkled in the light as she held the walnut close to the tall brass-columned lamp at one end of the desk. Imelda wondered if, to a man, those white, jewelled fingers would seem alluringly feminine.

"It's a pretty little piece, I suppose," said Beatrix, after a moment. "It doesn't appeal to me personally. You know my feelings on this subject, Charles. I consider it so much better, from every point of view, to invest in one first-

102

class piece, rather than an assortment of five-guinea trifles."

"Is that your professional valuation?" he enquired.

She shrugged. "I daresay it would cost more in Bond Street, or considerably less in a back street junk shop. It has very little intrinsic value, even if the fittings are silver gilt."

Again the door opened. This time it was Mrs. Wingfield who came in. "Ah, there you are, Charles. Someone called Melford is on the telephone for you. Robert Melford, I think he said."

"Melford?" Charles repeated, frowning. His expression cleared. "Oh, yes, I remember . . ."

As he spoke, Imelda leaned forward, took the walnut from Beatrix's open palm, and slipped it inside her bag before Mrs. Wingfield could catch sight of it.

"I'll take the call here. Would you excuse me for a short time?" said Charles, glancing from Beatrix to Imelda.

They returned to the drawing-room with their hostess, and by the time he reappeared Imelda was in conversation with a woman who, having inherited an oak dresser, had conceived an interest in Staffordshire Blue plates.

It was a subject which, at another time, Imelda would have discussed with enthusiasm. But as Charles came back to the drawing-room and, after glancing in her direction, turned to join a group which included Beatrix, her cheeks burned with the mortifying conviction that he thought she had been trying to exploit his ignorance of his grandmother's speciality.

Did Beatrix honestly consider the walnut to be worth only five pounds? Or had she been trying to discredit Imelda both as a dealer and a person?

I don't believe she came to the library to use the en-

103

cyclopaedia. I believe she saw Charles and me leaving the room, and followed us out of curiosity, thought Imelda.

"... don't you agree, Miss Calthorpe?" the woman beside her was saying.

With an effort, Imelda brought her thoughts back to transfer ware, and managed to cover up her impolite absence of mind.

At eleven, the local doctor and his wife, and a couple who lived at Bury St. Edmunds, took their leave. Imelda followed their example.

"So early?" said Mrs. Wingfield. "But of course you have to be up early in the morning, don't you, my dear? I'll come to the shop tomorrow to look at the things you are keeping aside for me. Ah, Charles" – as he appeared at her side– "Imelda is leaving. Would you see her safely on her way?"

"With pleasure," said Charles.

In the circumstances it was an equivocal answer, although there was nothing in his expression to confirm Imelda's suspicion that he meant it equivocally.

"I think I'd better run you home if this will be your first experience of night driving," he said, as they reached her car and she produced her key ring. "I can come back across country," he added, before she could object. "It's only a mile by the footpath, and it's a lovely night."

"It's kind of you – but quite unnecessary," Imelda said firmly. "Your other guests aren't leaving yet, and your grandmother would wonder where you were."

"She'll guess I've taken you home. You may be able to drive in that dress, but you certainly couldn't change a wheel in it. If you don't want anyone else to drive your car, I'll come as a passenger." And, having opened the driver's door for her, he walked round the back of the car and got in from the other side.

There was nothing to do but submit. Silently fuming, Imelda took her place behind the wheel, closed the door, and switched on the engine. She wished now that she had surrendered to his offer to drive. If his real reason for accompanying her was to talk about the walnut, she would never be able to concentrate on her driving, and she had not yet reached the comfortable stage of being able to change gear without thinking about it.

They were half way down the moonlit drive when Charles stretched out a hand to switch on the headlights. Perversely, she found his silence more aggravating than the derisive quip which was no doubt on the tip of his tongue.

The car was too small for anyone of his height. When they turned out of the gates on to the road, the action of changing gear caused her knuckles to brush against his leg. If it had been Sam beside her, the accidental contact would not have bothered her. But being in a small car with Charles was like being caged with a Great Dane of uncertain temper.

He was silent until they were approaching the turning which led into the colony of bungalows. "If you'll drop me at the corner, I can cut across the churchyard," he said.

She slowed and steered to the kerb. But when the car was at a standstill, he made no move to get out. She had put on the handbrake but left the engine running. Deliberately, Charles reached across the wheel and switched off the motor.

CHAPTER IV

WHATEVER Imelda expected, and several possibilities flashed through her mind in the seconds after the engine fell silent, it did not occur to her that his next action would be to slip his hand inside his dinner jacket and produce a long envelope.

"Six fivers," he said, handing it to her. "I assume you would rather have notes than a cheque?"

"Y – you mean you want to buy the walnut after all? In spite of what Mrs. Otley said about it?"

"I would be guided by Beatrix if I were buying porcelain or eighteenth-century furniture, but she isn't knowledgeable in the field where my grandmother's interests lie."

"Nor am I."

"Possibly not, but you know more about it than Beatrix. And I know enough about you to trust your judgment in this instance."

It was absurd to feel so pleased, so warmed. Dismayed by the sudden importance to her of his good opinion, she said: "I don't know what I've done to earn your confidence. It isn't long since you had a very poor opinion of my judgment."

"I have never doubted your integrity, merely your ability to survive in a tough line of business."

Perhaps it was merely incipient cramp which made him alter his position, shifting sideways and placing his right arm along the top of both backrests.

"Nevertheless I should feel happier if you had the thing valued by someone else," she said, rather breathlessly. "There must be a dealer in the county whose opinion would be authoritative."

"Your opinion is good enough for me."

Charles held out his palm and, after a moment's hesitation, she reached for her bag which was on the ledge above the dashboard, and gave him the walnut.

"Thank you."

"Thank *you*," she countered, tucking the banknotes away. Tomorrow she would take them to old Mrs. Titchwell.

"Now that's settled . . ." Again Charles moved.

At the touch of his hand on her shoulder, Imelda tensed. She couldn't help it.

". . . I'd better not delay you any further," he concluded, in a markedly dry tone. "As my grandmother remarked, you have to be up early in the morning, and so do I. Goodnight, Imelda."

It was clear from his voice that he guessed what had been in her mind, and equally clear that nothing could have been further from his own thoughts. His touch had been accidental, caused by the smallness of the car and the tallness of the man.

"Goodnight, Charles," she answered, as he opened the door and unfolded his long legs. Even to use his name gave her a small pang of pleasure.

As she had been on the night of Imelda's date with Sam, Mrs. Walsham was awake, and eager to hear a full account of the dinner party. Imelda described the food, and the other guests, and all the time her mind was on Charles, visualising him walking through the moonlit churchyard, past the imposing Wingfield vault and the inconspicuous grave of her great-aunt.

Presently, as she was undressing, she wondered if by now he was escorting Beatrix to the lodge cottage. Good

107

manners would oblige him to see her home, even if in-
clination did not do so. As clearly as if she were watching
a film, Imelda imagined the two of them strolling down
the long tree-lined avenue from the Hall to the main
gates. The only thing which her imagination failed to supply was their conversation.

When she arrived at the shop the next morning, there was
a letter with a Sussex postmark among the mail on the
doormat. But it was not from Sebastian Ellough. It had
been written by the matron of the private nursing home
where Sebastian had spent his last years and where, three
days ago, he had died.

Imelda was deeply upset by this news. In spite of Sebastian's advanced age, he had retained all his faculties
and she had expected him to go on for years. She was filled
with regret that she had not visited him more often, although the matron referred to the pleasure her regular
letters had given the old man.

She felt distraite and depressed all morning, although
she made an effort to seem normally cheerful to two trade
callers and one private customer.

It was nearly lunch time when Sam called. She was
busy upstairs when the bell jangled and, seeing his van
from the window, she finished what she was doing before
she went down.

"You've sold the watch, I see," he remarked, looking
up from the specimen case in which she displayed small
valuable items.

Imelda looked blankly at him. "No, I haven't."

He glanced round the shop. "Where've you put it?"

"Nowhere . . . it's in the display case."

But the pretty enamelled fob watch which Sam had
sold to her the week before was no longer where she had

seen it earlier that morning. "It's gone," she exclaimed, in a hollow voice. "Oh, Sam – it must have been stolen. I *know* it was there when I arrived."

Sam looked grim. "How many customers have you had this morning?"

"Only three. Two dealers, and a woman looking for piqué jewellery. She wasn't the type to steal things."

"Who were the dealers?"

She told him.

"Then it must have been her. Have a look to see what else is missing."

To Imelda's dismay, she had also lost a scarf pin and a locket. "She must have grabbed them when I went to the back door to speak to old Mrs. Medlar," she said, feeling slightly sick.

"You left her alone in here? A stranger?" Sam ejaculated.

"Only for a moment. She seemed so nice ... so respectable."

He groaned and slapped his palm against his forehead. "Shoplifters generally do, stupid. If they didn't, they wouldn't get away with it so often."

Imelda bit her lip. She remembered that when she had returned from the rear of the premises the woman had been studying a framed sampler. They had chatted about it for some minutes, and then the woman had glanced at her watch and said that she must hurry home but would call again the following week. She had smiled at Imelda, full of friendliness. And all the time the watch and the other two pieces must have been in her bag or her pocket.

"Hey, don't cry," exclaimed Sam, seeing the sudden quivering of her lips. "I didn't mean to blast at you ... I'm sorry."

"It's not you. It's her," she said chokily, blinking back tears.

She might have regained her control if he had not touched her. But his arm round her back was fatally comforting, and when he said kindly, "Poor love ... never mind," she hid her face against his shoulder as she might have turned to her stepfather, had he been there.

Sam patted her back, and listened to her rather incoherent explanation of why she had been less alert than usual that morning. In the middle of it, someone opened the shop door, apologised and withdrew.

"Who was that?" asked Imelda, quickly wiping her cheeks with her fingers before she looked towards the door.

"Don't know his name. Seen him around. Tall, dark bloke. Thought we were snogging, I suppose," said Sam, with an amused shrug.

A car passed the window, pulling away from the kerb. It was gone too swiftly for the man at the wheel to be recognisable. But the car was a big silver saloon like the one Charles drove.

As Imelda walked back to her digs that night, she felt the day had been a perfect example of the saying – troubles never come singly.

Of the three unpleasant happenings which had hit her in rapid succession, it was the theft she minded least. Her sense of loss concerning Sebastian would persist, she knew, for a long time. But it would be a gentle sadness for someone who had lived long and fully; not the bitter grief she had known when her father was killed. The thing which weighed on her most heavily – yet which was by far the most trivial – was the possibility that Charles did think Sam had been kissing her.

Charles had not returned to the shop in the afternoon, and she longed to know what had brought him there in the first place. Had he changed his mind about the walnut? Had he wanted merely to see her? If he had, no doubt he didn't any more. He was not the sort of man to dally with a girl who was dallying with someone else, particularly someone of Sam's sort.

The fact that it was probably just as well that Charles' interest had been nipped in the bud was not a comfort. The matter continued to trouble her, and she was still brooding about it when she travelled home for the week-end.

Yet from the moment she arrived at Liverpool Street Station, and made her way to the Underground, she began to realise that London was home no longer. It was nice to see her family, but there was a difference between a homecoming and an agreeable visit. Her home, the centre of her world, was in Norfolk now; and when Monday morning came, and she stood in the crowded tube train, disliking the press of bodies and the staleness and smokiness of the atmosphere, which once she would scarcely have noticed, she found she was not sorry to be leaving the capital.

Inevitably, her arrival at the railway station reminded her of her first journey into East Anglia, and her meeting with Mrs. Wingfield. And then the thought of Charles, which all weekend she had shunned like a dieter resisting sweets or a smoker resisting cigarettes, became stronger than her resolution. As she sat by the window, watching her fellow travellers scanning the compartments for unoccupied corner seats, her mind reverted to the question: Why had he come to the shop that day?

So preoccupied was she with Charles-in-imagination that when Charles-in-reality walked past her window, checked his stride, and turned to look back at whoever had called him by his surname, Imelda thought for an instant that by sheer force of mind she had superimposed his dark face on a stranger of similar height and build.

The centre window was open and, as she stared at him, another man hurried along from the direction of the ticket barrier, and said, "Hello, Wingfield. This is a stroke of luck. I've been wanting to have a word with you about ■■."

The drone of a passing electric trolley muffled the rest of his remark.

Perhaps Charles sensed someone watching him. As the short man continued speaking to him, he turned his head slightly and met Imelda's startled gaze. For a moment, she thought he was going to cut her. There was no mistaking the coldness of his expression. Then, with the stiffest of nods, he turned away and walked out of sight with the shorter man.

The two-hour journey seemed interminable. Imelda tried to concentrate on a book about New Hall porcelain but, engrossing as it was, it could not make her forget Charles' presence further down the train.

On arrival at Norwich she fled along the platform to the refuge of the women's cloakroom where she lurked for fifteen minutes to avoid any possibility of a second encounter which would force him to offer her a lift.

Fortunately this subterfuge did not cause her to miss the bus, but later it made her angry with herself. What an idiotic way to behave! If he had offered and she had accepted a lift home, it would have been an opportunity to disabuse him of false impressions about her relationship with Sam.

The following weekend she was able to leave Mrs. Walsham's bungalow, and move to her own house which now had a galley-sized kitchen in what had formerly been the scullery, and a bathroom in the smallest bedroom.

"I shall miss you," said her landlady regretfully, when Imelda paid her final week's board. "It's the evenings on my own I don't like."

"Why not have another lodger?"

"No, I don't think I will, not now I'm helping you at the shop. I don't want to take on too much."

"A lodger would be more profitable," said Imelda. "Don't be embarrassed about telling me if you want to give up the shopminding."

"Oh, I don't, dear," said Mrs. Walsham firmly. "I enjoy it too much. It takes me out of myself. I only wish I'd taken an interest years ago when everything was so much cheaper."

In spite of Mrs. Walsham's fears that she would be nervous sleeping alone in the bedroom above the front parlour, Imelda felt no trepidation as she climbed the stairs on her first night in her new home. However eerie the upper rooms might have been in Miss Partridge's time, they were not so now. Indeed Imelda's bedroom, with its walls and ceiling papered with a red and white *toile de Jouy* of milkmaids and shepherds, its floor close-carpeted, and the ornate brass bedstead set off by a crocheted coverlet which, after being boiled, was as snowy as the snowflakes on which it was patterned, was so pretty and cosy that for some time she sat up in bed, admiring the existing décor and planning such finishing touches as a needlework rug, and perhaps a small Eaton Hall chair and a set of hanging shelves.

A few days after her removal, she was in Norwich, queueing for fish at a stall on the fringe of the fruit market, when Mrs. Wingfield came by.

"Imelda! How are you, my dear? Did you wonder what

had become of me? I've been staying in Cambridge fo
a few days. I called at the shop this morning, as a matte
of fact, and Mrs. Walsham said you were in the city.
was hoping our paths might cross."

"Did you find some nice things in Cambridge?" Imeld
enquired.

"For the collection, d'you mean? Yes, I came hom
with several treasures. One of them is in my bag now
Come and have lunch with me, and I'll show it to you.

Imelda demurred, but Mrs. Wingfield insisted. "M
friends in Cambridge are not collectors, so I've had n
one with whom I could gloat over my finds. You'll appre
ciate them, I know."

She took Imelda to her club where, it being rathe
early to eat, they had drinks in the bar beforehand. Ther
were not many other people present and, having said goo
morning to a couple of acquaintances, Mrs. Wingfiel
steered Imelda to a sofa, and began to delve in her bag

It was a rather cool day for early July, and they wer
both wearing summer trouser suits. Imelda's was scarle
paired with a striped matelot top. Mrs. Wingfield's sui
was silver-grey linen over a caramel silk shirt. Watchin
her, Imelda thought admiringly that Elizabeth Wingfiel
was an excellent example of how to grow old gracefully
Although her fine dry skin was very lined, and she ha
given up using cosmetics other than powder, she still use
a delightful scent, and her slim figure and up-to-dat
choice of clothes – her satchel and shoes were in the sam
casual style as Imelda's – made her seem younger than he
years.

"This I couldn't resist, although it was rather expens
ive," she said, unwrapping the tissue protecting a silver
gilt bodkin case.

Imelda was studying the design through her pocke

glass when, to her dismay, Mrs. Wingfield remarked, "Hello, Charles. You're early, too. I met Imelda and persuaded her to join us."

Her grandson looked down at her guest, his expression unfathomable. "Hello, Imelda, how are you?"

"Fine. How are you?" she returned, outwardly calm. Inwardly, she felt anything but composed. It had not crossed her mind that Charles might be joining them, and although his grandmother's presence relieved the encounter of much of its awkwardness, it did not do so completely.

The two women being already supplied with dry sherry, Charles signalled to the steward and asked for lager for himself. He sat down in the chair at his grandmother's end of the sofa, and crossed his legs.

Resuming her study of the bodkin case, Imelda was conscious of him watching her, and was grateful for the impulse which had caused her to spend the previous evening attending to her hair and nails. She might so easily have spent the time wire-wooling or stripping, and although it never bothered her if Sam, or other men, saw her looking less than her best, with Charles it was important to be immaculate. Until recently she would have pretended to herself that this was merely a matter of added self-assurance. Now she had to admit there was only one reason why a girl, not normally vain, suddenly minded very much how she looked in the eyes of one man.

It was while they were finishing their lunch with strawberries and cream that Mrs. Wingfield gave Imelda the opportunity she had hoped for by remarking, "You've had all my news, but said very little of your affairs. Has business been good lately?"

"This week has been good. Last week was rather unpleasant." Imelda told her of Sebastian's death, and of the thefts. She looked across the table at Charles who was

115

sitting opposite her. "I believe you called at the shop that morning?"

"Yes, but I could see it was an inopportune moment, so I went away."

Imelda turned back to his grandmother. "Charles is being tactful. I'm afraid the truth is that I was 'giving way to emotion', as they say in Victorian novelettes. I'm not a weepy person normally, but having something stolen by someone you've liked the look of is a hateful sensation, and coming on top of the news about Sebastian . . ." She left the sentence in the air.

"My dear child, how wretched for you. I *am* sorry," said Mrs. Wingfield concernedly. "Well, really, Charles, I do think you might at least have stayed to offer Imelda your handkerchief. To turn tail –"

"Imelda wasn't alone. She was already being comforted."

"Oh, by Mrs. Walsham, I suppose. But if she was at the shop, how did the other woman manage to –"

"No, Sam Mutford was with me," said Imelda. "It was he who noticed the watch was missing. Which reminds me, why did you say to me once that I shouldn't have too much to do with him, Charles?"

"The name Mutford is not synonymous with respectability in this district," he replied, with a slight shrug.

"Indeed it is not!" agreed Mrs. Wingfield wryly. "The trouble that family have caused. A most unruly clan! However, there may be exceptions. I don't recall a Sam Mutford being brought before the Bench in my time."

Imelda explained the nature of her connection with Sam. "I'm sure *he* is completely honest. It's most unfair to tar him with the family brush. But for their reputation, he would be engaged to the girl who was chosen Carnival Queen last week," she added. "Unfortunately her mother has managed to put her off him, and now she's going about with an Inland Revenue clerk who may be more respectable, but who's not half the man Sam is."

"As Carnival Queens usually have very little to recommend them, beyond a pretty face and good figure, I should think he may be better off without her," remarked Mrs. Wingfield. "Talking of carnivals and other summer festivities, I wonder if you would care to come to a reception at the Castle Museum next week, Imelda?"

An hour later, as she was driving home, Imelda realised that she was no wiser about the cause of Charles' visit to the shop. But at least *he* knew now the reason why Sam had had his arm around her, and surely her reference to Diane must have made it clear that there was nothing sentimental in her own relationship with Sam?

On the evening of the reception, Imelda was ready some time before Mrs. Wingfield was due to call for her. She had had a new dress made at a shop in Norwich which sold unusual fabrics and made them up in whatever style customers wanted. She had chosen a lovely dull silk, the colour of bronze, and had sketched a plain, long-sleeved style to which, at home, she had added a collar and cuffs of ivory lace which someone had brought to Victoriana in a bundle of old trimmings.

From her bedroom window, Imelda could see the junction of the main road with the road which led to the Hall. But it was Charles' car, not Mrs. Wingfield's, which presently came into view. Imelda had not realised he was coming with them. Perhaps he was not. Perhaps he had a different engagement, and was merely chauffeuring them to and fro.

It was too mild an evening for a wrap to be necessary. Taking her bag from the bed, she went quickly down-

stairs to check that the back door was bolted. As she le
herself out of the front door, Charles was parking th
car alongside the kerb. But there was no one with him
Puzzled, Imelda turned to lock the door. By the time sh
had put the key in her bag, he was walking round the bon
net to join her on the pavement.

"I came early in the expectation of having to wait a
least ten minutes, but evidently I misjudged you," he said

"Indeed you did. I can't bear unpunctuality. Where'
your grandmother?"

"She hasn't been very well today, and she doesn't fee
up to an evening out. You have no objection to going t
the reception with me, I hope?"

"No, of course not. But had you intended to come witl
us? Or are you standing in so as not to disappoint me'
If so, it's very kind of you . . . but quite unnecessary."

His left eyebrow tilted upwards. "Is that an obliqu
way of conveying that in the circumstances you woulc
rather not go?"

"That was not what I meant at all." *And you know it*
she added mentally.

"Good, because Grandmother is expecting a detailec
description of the occasion, and according to her I'm a
very indifferent reporter," he said, opening the nearsid
door of the car for her.

"What's wrong with Mrs. Wingfield? Nothing serious
I hope?" said Imelda, when he slid behind the wheel.

"No, no – a headache and general lassitude. She doe
too much. Instead of resting after lunch, she weeds. In
stead of having breakfast in bed, she gets up at seven tc
write letters to friends and relations who hardly ever
write to her. I've tried to make her slow down, but she's
incorrigible."

The walls of Norwich Castle were tinged with apricot

reflections from the western sky when they reached their destination. People in evening dress were converging on the Castle from all directions, dawdling to enjoy the sunset, the lingering warmth of the hot day, and the unwonted quiet of the city bereft of its heavy daytime traffic.

The Castle stood on the summit of a great grass-covered mound shaded by mature trees. As Charles and Imelda strolled across the bridge which spanned the public gardens at the foot of the mound, it was evident that most of the other guests arriving for the reception had at least a nodding acquaintance with each other.

"I suppose you know most of these people," she said.

"Not as many as Grandmother does. I don't take much part in the local social life. I prefer my parties *à deux*," said Charles in a tone which, although she knew he was teasing, sent a queer little shiver down her spine.

He might not have as wide an acquaintance as Mrs. Wingfield, but there were many people who looked at him with interested recognition, and at her with curiosity, Imelda noticed, when they had shaken hands with the Lord Mayor and the other people in the receiving line.

The first person she recognised was Beatrix, who at the same instant spotted Imelda and gave her a wintry smile which changed to a stare of surprise when she saw Imelda's tall companion.

Beatrix murmured something to the women with whom she had been chatting, and came to speak to them. She was wearing a 'Thirties dress of flowered chiffon with bishop sleeves, a tiered skirt and a knot of chiffon flowers tucked through the belt. She looked graceful, and noticeably chic amid the preponderance of too-tight Lurex.

"Good evening, Miss Calthorpe. I didn't expect to see you here, Charles. I thought you loathed these affairs? But I daresay you don't like Elizabeth to drive herself at night, and Miss Calthorpe is a novice, I believe."

"Grandmother is having an early night after a tirin
day, and Imelda and I have dropped in on our way to
dinner party," he said pleasantly.

"Oh . . . I see."

But she doesn't, thought Imelda. And neither do]
What dinner party?

She had no opportunity to ask him. When, after som
rather forced pleasantries, Beatrix drifted away, a tal
upright, elderly woman in a dress which appeared to be
genuine relic of the 'Thirties, not merely a fashion copy
bore down on Charles with a loud, "Hello, old chap, ho
are you? Where's Elizabeth? I want a word with her."

For the third time that evening Charles explained th
reason for his grandmother's absence.

"Hmph, not like Elizabeth to give way to a headache,
said the tall woman. "Hope she isn't beginning to crac
up. You ought to get married, you know, Charle:
Shouldn't be difficult for you to find a suitable wife nov
Must be any number of nice girls who'd be only too de
lighted to take you on."

"You mean now that I stand in my brother's shoes?
His voice held no expression, but the hardening of his ja
was not lost on Imelda, although the tall woman seeme
oblivious of it.

Her attention had shifted to Imelda. "Are you the Ben
gates' youngest girl?"

"Miss Calthorpe is an antique dealer from London,
said Charles, introducing the tall woman as Mrs. Baw
burgh.

"How d'you do? You're not with Sotheby's, by an
chance?" enquired Mrs. Bawburgh.

"No."

"Pity. I've a Chinese pot which I'm told I ought to hav
120

valued. Hideous thing, but it could be frightfully valuable apparently. Do you know about Oriental stuff?"

"I'm afraid not. It's a very specialised field."

Mrs. Bawburgh turned back to Charles. "I wanted to ask Elizabeth if she would open our fête on Saturday. Lady Raynham has broken her leg. Most inconvenient of her! But I expect Elizabeth will come to the rescue. I'll telephone first thing in the morning." She moved away.

Seeing the stormy light in Charles' eyes, Imelda said lightly, "Is it a compliment to be mistaken for one of the Bengate girls?"

"I haven't met them. As I told you earlier, I don't socialise more than I must," he replied rather curtly.

"Because you're annoyed with Mrs. Bawburgh, there's no need to bite my head off," she retorted, in the tone she might have used to her brother in one of his grumpy moods.

Charles turned a glacial grey gaze on her, and for an instant she quailed.

"You're right. I apologise." The icy glint left his eyes, replaced by a look less daunting but equally disturbing. "Let's go and look at the Cotmans, shall we?" He took hold of her arm to steer her through the increasing throng in the Rotunda.

There were fewer people in the picture galleries. As Imelda had discovered many weeks ago, the Castle contained a fine collection of pictures by the famous Norwich School of landscape painters. Now she found that not only did Charles share her preference for watercolours rather than oils, but that her favourite landscape was also his favourite.

"Why did you tell Beatrix we were on our way to a dinner party?" she asked him presently.

He turned from gazing at a Girtin. "Was I unwise to

121

assume that you would dine with me afterwards?"

"You mean . . . alone with you?"

"Only in the sense that there won't be anyone else at our table. We're unlikely to have the restaurant to ourselves."

"I – I should be delighted," she answered, her throat oddly tight.

Less than an hour later, somewhere in the country to the south of the city Charles parked the car in the yard of a weatherboarded water-mill. In the late summer dusk they lingered to look at the mill stream before entering the building where, in the restaurant overlooking the river, a candle in a shining glass storm shade shed its soft light over each table.

"I gather you don't rate respectability as one of the essential attributes of a husband," he said unexpectedly, between the melon and the lamb cutlets.

"What makes you say that?" she asked, startled by the abrupt change of subject. They had been discussing a seascape on the wall near their table.

"It was the impression you gave when you were telling my grandmother about Mutford's ex-girl-friend over lunch last week."

"It depends what one means by respectability. I believe it's important to be honest and clean and punctual," she answered thoughtfully. "But I don't think people who work in offices are necessarily more eligible than people who work with their hands. Surely the important factor is not how much someone earns, or how secure their job is, but whether they really enjoy what they do for a living. Can anyone *enjoy* totting up other people's taxes or filing forms? When I worked in an insurance office I never looked forward to the days as I do now, and I'm certain that Sam is a much happier person than Melvyn."

"Are you completely happy living here? You don't miss London at all? You don't feel any urge to discover other places . . . other countries?"

"I should like to go abroad, certainly. Perhaps next year, if the profits will stand it, I shall be able to have a foreign holiday. You're a much-travelled person, so I'm told. Where would you recommend me to go the first time?"

"The places I prefer are not very suitable for a girl on her own. If you wanted a busman's holiday, France would be better than Spain, where most of the so-called antiques are made of plastic." He drank some wine, eyeing her over the rim of the glass. As he replaced it on the table, he said, "What would you do if you had to live somewhere where there were no antique shops and nothing to collect?"

"There's always *something* to collect . . . old bottles, shells, even pebbles. Nowhere could be more frustrating than London – for a collector who hasn't any money!" she answered dryly.

It was only a little after eleven when he stopped the car outside her door. As she took her latch-key from her bag, he held out his hand to take it from her and unlock the door. She was about to invite him in for coffee, and to ask his opinion of some old books she had bought a few days before, when he forestalled her by saying crisply, "I won't come in. This village is a hotbed of gossip and you don't want to risk your reputation. Goodnight, Imelda. I hope you'll dine with me again some time."

"I should like to. Thank you for tonight, Charles. Goodnight." She held out her hand and felt again the firm clasp she remembered from the day of her great-aunt's funeral.

In the kitchen, making coffee for one, she could not
123

help feeling a certain disappointment that the evening had ended so early. Had he meant his suggestion of a future date, or had that been merely a politeness? "Some time" was extremely vague. Perhaps she had bored him. And yet there had been moments during the evening when she had felt the rapport between them almost as tangibly as, at other moments, she had felt his fingers on her elbow.

The following morning, while Imelda was hanging up a large oval earthenware goose dish with the Minton impressed mark for 1859, Beatrix called on her.

Imelda was surprised to see her, and even more surprised when, without knowing the price, Beatrix said she would buy the dish.

"I didn't think Victorian pottery was your line of country," Imelda remarked, as she lifted it down and detached the wire hanger.

"It isn't really, but a customer has asked me to find her two or three chargers to use as trays for cocktail snacks," Beatrix explained. "How much are these?" – picking up a boxed set of silver Art Nouveau buttons.

"There should be a price ticket on the underside of the box."

Beatrix found it, and bought the buttons. As she turned her attention to a watercolour of Venice, Imelda's kettle began to whistle.

"Would you care for some coffee?" she asked.

"How kind. Yes, thank you, I should," Beatrix said affably.

They drank it in the back parlour. Presently, watching Imelda wrapping the charger, the older woman said, "There's something I think you should know about Charles and myself."

Imelda stiffened. She had felt in her bones that the visit was not a business call.

"Shortly before you came to Norfolk, Charles asked me to marry him."

Imelda was fastening the parcel with sticky tape, an occupation which helped her to conceal her dismay. Then dismay gave place to incredulity. "And you refused him?" she asked sceptically.

"Yes – and now I wish I hadn't," Beatrix admitted. "I feel I should tell you the circumstances, because I gather that Charles is making a set at you, and I wouldn't like it to lead to unhappiness for you."

"Charles isn't making a set at me. We attended the reception together merely because Mrs. Wingfield cried off at the last moment."

"Has it occurred to you that Charles may have suggested that she should absent herself?"

"I think it's highly unlikely. Why did you refuse his proposal?"

"My first marriage was a mistake. We were on the brink of separation when my husband was killed in a motorway accident. Anyone who has been through an unhappy marriage thinks twice before risking another partnership. To marry Charles involves taking on his brother's children. I'm not good with children . . . any children. They don't take to me, and to be candid I'm not much interested in them. Nor am I particularly domesticated, and Elizabeth has said several times that when Charles marries she'll hand over the running of that huge house. It's become too much for her, and in a different sense it would be too much for me. I should have to give up the shop, and that's something I don't wish to do – even for Charles."

"Do you love him?" Imelda asked bluntly.

"If I didn't, would I be here, confiding my feelings to you?"

"Surely it would be more effective to confide them to Charles?"

"Charles is angry that I didn't accept him immediately. He's an extremely attractive, eligible man and I don't suppose it crossed his mind that I wouldn't fall into his arms. I only wish I had – or at least had asked for time to think it over. Like a fool, I turned him down flat, which is a blow to any man's pride, even to a man with Charles's self-confidence."

"Then surely the remedy is for you to shelve your pride and tell him how you feel now," Imelda suggested.

"Yes, but that's easier said than done. Charles is deliberately being as unapproachable as possible, and every time I nerve myself to speak to him, I'm overcome with the fear that *he* may have changed his mind too. It was with the object of speaking to him that I followed him to the library on the night of Elizabeth's dinner party. When I found you with him, I had to make an excuse about wanting to refer to the encyclopaedia."

The doorbell rang, and Imelda excused herself to go and attend to another customer who turned out to be a dealer from Essex in search of automata. While she was talking to him, Beatrix paused on her way out to say, "I've left a cheque on the table. I must go or I shall be late for an appointment." With a nod to the man from Essex and a smile for Imelda she departed.

The cheque, as Imelda discovered presently, was made out for the full marked price of the two things Beatrix had bought. The fact that she had not asked for, or deducted, the customary trade discount confirmed Imelda's opinion that they had been bought chiefly to put her in a good mood before the main purpose of the call was broached.

Thinking over everything Beatrix had told her, Imelda was not convinced of the truth of her claim that Charles had asked her to marry him. At the same time she could not dismiss the possibility that it might be true. The thought that Charles might be using her as a pawn disturbed her peace of mind all that day.

"And if and when he asks me for another date, I can't ask *him* if he did propose without betraying Beatrix's confidence and putting her in a shaming position if he did not," she thought uneasily.

On Sunday, Sam took her to an open-air market in the next county. She was filling the kettle when he arrived. "Hello, Sam. I'm just going to make a flask of coffee. We might be glad of a hot drink as the weather has suddenly become so chilly. Or is there a coffee stall on the market?"

"There were a couple of chip vans the last time I was down there. I don't know about a coffee stall. Anyhow, a flask is a good idea."

Turning to plug in the kettle, she glanced at him and saw there was something different about him. It wasn't merely that he had been to the barber and had his hair trimmed or that he was wearing new navy-blue needle-cord jeans and a dark plum-coloured sweater. It was something she could not define. Her glance became a puzzled stare which made Sam smile.

"You've shaved off your whiskers!" she exclaimed.

Of the Genghis Khan moustache which ever since she had known him had framed his firm jaw and given him a rather wild, fierce appearance, nothing was left but a band of skin paler than the rest of his face.

127

"Don't you think it's an improvement?"

"I'm not sure. Yes ... no ... I don't know. What made you do it?"

"I thought you didn't like it," he answered.

The implication of this statement made her turn away quickly to busy herself spooning coffee powder into the vacuum flask. The safest response seemed to be: "What do your family think about it?"

"They weren't up when I left home. I only took it off this morning."

They arrived at the airfield where the market was held at about a quarter to twelve. Officially the market did not open to the public until one o'clock, but already a score of private cars were parked along the edge of the main runway. The traders' vehicles and their stalls were arranged along the opposite edge of the runway and down its centre, enclosing an area about half a mile long and thirty or forty feet wide. Most of the junk stalls were grouped together and, as Sam had warned her on the way there, most of the objects for sale were of little interest or value. But while Sam was chatting to an acquaintance Imelda spotted a pair of pictures propped against the trestle of a stall which made her bend down to examine them.

"You don't want those old things, do you?" said Sam, coming to peer over her shoulder.

"I rather like them," she said. The black frames with their narrow gold-leafed liners were battered and dulled, but behind the dirty, fly-spotted glass the coloured prints – if they were prints – had a naïve charm which appealed to her.

The stall-holder, scenting her interest, said, "At a pound the pair you can't go wrong, love."

She paid him a pound and Sam put the pictures in the van. Then they strolled to the far end of the market, past

128

stalls selling cut-price carpets and "seconds" crockery, past a man selling ironing-board covers and another selling paintbrushes, past a candy floss kiosk and a shrimp stand. Bed-linen, potted plants, peppermints, melons, rustic furniture for gardens – the market offered a wide variety of wares.

To the south of the long-disused runway lay a cornfield and, beyond it, a rolling panorama of oaks and elms and hawthorn hedges reminiscent of a landscape by Constable. But although the sun had come out, the wind flapping the awnings of the larger stalls had an unseasonable nip in it, and Imelda was glad of the thick jersey under her car coat.

"Cold?" asked Sam, taking her hand.

"Only at the edges. How warm you are!"

"What you need is a hamburger." Still holding her hand, he joined the short queue at the hamburger van.

The crowd in the lane between the stalls was increasing rapidly now. Judging from the snatches of conversation which Imelda overheard as she waited for Sam to buy the hamburgers, many of the people arriving would have spent the day at the coast, had it been warmer.

"I think those two pictures I bought might just possibly be early gouaches," she said, in a lowered voice, as they strolled along eating the hamburgers. Her left hand was still clasped firmly in his, and there seemed no casual way to disengage it.

"You mean they could be valuable?"

"Oh, Sam, don't be so mercenary. It isn't what they're worth which is important to me. It's their possible age which is interesting, and the fact that – if they *are* gouaches – I recognised them when a much more experienced dealer priced them at fifty pence each."

"I'd have sold them for half that," said Sam. "What

129

d'you say they're called? Gwarsh?"

She spelt the word for him. "That's the French term. The English is 'body colour'. It's watercolour with Chinese white added to make it opaque. I don't really know a great deal about it, except that it was more popular on the Continent than here, and I once fell in love with a painting of Naples from the sea which the dealer told me was a gouache."

"I hope you're right, but I have a nasty feeling you've wasted a quid on a couple of Edwardian coloured prints."

"Have you ever thought of taking a stall here?" asked Imelda, as they joined the crowd round a London trader selling bags.

Sam shook his head. "Selling the stuff is no problem. Finding it is the headache nowadays. How about a trip to the Portobello market next Saturday? They say you can buy cheaper up there than in the provinces."

"Yes, I think that's true," she agreed. "There are so many dealers all together that they have to be more competitive. But it costs over a fiver to get there, Sam."

"Not if we go by road and take a packed lunch. If we set off at seven, we should be in London by ten. Even if we didn't buy much, it would make a change, don't you think?"

Imelda deliberated. Supposing she agreed to Sam's suggestion and then, tomorrow, Charles invited her to go out with him the following Saturday? Was a day at the Portobello worth the risk of forgoing an outing with Charles?

Before she had made up her mind, she was surprised to notice Henry Wingfield wandering among the passersby. Some distance behind the boy came Charles and Beatrix, flanked by Sophie and Fanny. The little girls were holding hands with the grown-ups, and Beatrix had one hand tucked in the crook of Charles's arm. The four of them looked so much like a handsome, happy family that Imelda had a sinking conviction that Beatrix *had* spoken the truth on her visit to the shop, and that, since then, the estrangement between her and Charles had been resolved.

It was Fanny who spotted Imelda and pointed her out to her uncle.

"Hello. Do you two come here every Sunday?" asked Beatrix, smiling, when the four adults had greeted each other. "Do you find you can pick up some bargains?"

"Now and again," answered Sam, visibly puzzled by her graciousness.

He was still holding hands with Imelda, and she saw Charles glance at their clasped hands with an absence of expression which was somehow more condemnatory than if he had shown disapproval. Beyond saying Hello and Goodbye, he did not address her. Beatrix did all the talking.

"Looks like it won't be long before her shop will be for sale," said Sam, when the others had moved out of earshot. "I can't see her staying in the trade when she's Mrs. Wingfield!"

"She wasn't wearing an engagement ring." Imelda knew she was clutching at a straw. There had been an unmistakable element of triumph in Beatrix's cordial manner.

Imelda had left a chicken casserole in the oven. After lunching with her, Sam extracted the rusty tacks from the backs of the pictures she had bought. Removed from their unpleasing frames, the paintings were unquestionably gouaches painted early in the nineteenth century.

The day before she and her daughter, and the grandchildren, set off for their holiday at Charles's cottage in Menorca, Mrs. Wingfield called at the shop to say goodbye.

That morning Imelda had been to a farmhouse where the farmer's wife wanted to sell an enormous and peculiarly hideous sideboard, dating from the 1930s, which Imelda had had to refuse as tactfully as possible. However, she had not come away empty-handed, for the woman had had several charming examples of blue and white transfer-printed earthenware languishing, unappreciated, in her pantry. And, as Imelda was passing through the kitchen, she had noticed that a cat bed beside the Aga was lined with a patchwork quilt.

"I've always longed for a patchwork quilt. I'm tempted to keep it for myself," she said, showing it to Mrs. Wingfield. "But it's rather large for a single bed."

"Put it in your bottom drawer, if girls have such things nowadays. In spite of being slept on by a cat, it's in good condition, and early patchwork is not easy to come by these days. Some of these designs are most attractive," said Mrs. Wingfield, examining the diamonds of sprigged cotton from which the centre of the quilt was made. "These red pieces round the edge are turkey twill. It isn't obtainable any more, but until about ten years ago there was an old-fashioned draper's in Norwich where they sold it for railway guards' flags. A pity the quilt isn't signed and dated. I should put it at 1860 or thereabouts." Suddenly, she switched her gaze to Imelda's face. "You look a little wan, my dear. A holiday would do you good. What are your plans?"

"I have none. My family are going camping in Scotland, but there's only room for the four of them in my stepfather's car. Perhaps in September I'll close the shop for a few days and go on a business-cum-pleasure trip

132

to Wales. The Welsh border is supposed to be a good hunting ground."

Mrs. Wingfield bought one or two small objects to put away in a drawer until Christmas. Then, to Imelda's surprise, she kissed her goodbye.

"I shall see you in six weeks' time, my dear. Take care of yourself. Don't hesitate to telephone Charles if you find yourself in any kind of difficulty."

In the afternoon a man with a foreign accent called at Victoriana. Among other things he was looking for paintings and, after warning him that they were not for sale, Imelda showed him the pair of gouaches. He at once made an offer for them, raising it to sixty pounds when she was not tempted by his first figure. When he had left, promising to call on her again on his next trip to England, she wondered if she had been a fool to turn down such a handsome profit. But since the pictures pleased her, regardless of their value, it seemed foolish to part with them too hurriedly. She decided to spare no expense on having them attractively re-framed.

"They'll be a good investment for my old age," she thought. It was a private joke she had with herself whenever she was tempted by something expensive. Only suddenly it wasn't funny any more. The possibility that she might always live alone sent a queer little chill through her. All through her growing up years she had taken for granted that some day in the future there would be marriage and children and someone with whom to share the delights and the difficulties of life. Perhaps it would not be like that. Perhaps she would always be Miss Calthorpe, the antique dealer, never Mrs. Somebody, wife and mother.

During the week that followed the weather was at its

133

summer worst, and Imelda's spirits were as overcast as the leaden sky. One day, as she was staring gloomily out of the shop window, she saw Charles on the other side of the road. He was wearing the ancient clothes and heavy rubber boots of the working farmer, but his long-legged stride and straight shoulders were noticeably different from the heavy movements of most farmers, and the pop-singers' hunch affected by the younger agricultural workers.

He did not look in the direction of Victoriana, and Imelda wondered if, when he came out of the post office, he might cross the street to call on her for a few minutes. She felt sure Mrs. Wingfield would have said to him, "Do keep an eye on Imelda, Charles."

But by the time he reappeared it had begun to rain. With a glance at the lowering sky, he moved swiftly in the direction of the car park.

A picture postcard from Menorca, showing a golden beach sheltered by a rocky headland and lapped by a pellucid turquoise sea, did nothing to raise her morale. In an effort to distract herself, she started to make a lampshade to go on a rose-painted washstand ewer which had lost its matching basin. Odd jugs of this kind could be picked up very cheaply, and she hoped that, if she could "lamp" them successfully, they might fetch five or six pounds.

One evening, when she had finished binding the wire frame with lampshade tape, and was beginning to pin on the pink silk cover, someone knocked on her back door. Thinking it was Sam, whom she had not seen for several days, she went to the door and found Charles standing outside.

"Good evening. Have I called at an awkward moment?"

"No . . . not at all. Please come in."

The back parlour was not at its tidiest, and nor was Im-

134

elda. She had been out all day, and was still wearing the sweater and jeans she had put on that morning.

"I see you've had a card from the island," said Charles, nodding at the postcard on the mantelpiece.

"Yes. They seem to be having a splendid time. Would you care for some coffee?"

"No, thank you."

"A drink, perhaps? There's sherry, beer or cider."

"Beer, please." He had the air of someone who does not intend to linger.

As she opened a can of chilled beer, and tipped some pretzels into a dish, Imelda reflected that five minutes ago, absorbed in the task of pinning silk, she had been at peace for a little while. Now Charles would stay for ten minutes and go on his way leaving her in a fresh state of turmoil.

Returning to the parlour, she said, "Have you any interesting news?"

He shook his head. "I had a letter from my grandmother, describing their journey to Barcelona. Otherwise I've been closeted in the library, catching up with a backlog of paperwork."

He looked as if he had been working hard ... overworking, she thought. The farmer's wife from whom she had bought the patchwork quilt had bemoaned the amount of paperwork, but Imelda was surprised that Charles found it necessary to burn the midnight oil. She would have expected him to have an efficient system worked out, and if necessary to employ a part-time secretary.

On the table near which he was sitting there were a number of small objects waiting to be cleaned and priced. Idly, he picked up an ivory paper-knife and examined the carving on it. Then, to Imelda's surprise, he raised it to eye-level and looked through the tiny hole in the handle. She would not have expected him to recognise the hole for what it was. His grandmother must have enlightened him. Several of Mrs. Wingfield's Victorian needle-cases had peepholes showing magnified views of the places where, long ago, they had been bought as souvenirs.

"Do you know the history of these things?" he asked.

She shook her head. "Only that they all seem to have been made in France. Even those, like the one you're holding, which are souvenirs of English resorts."

"No, they were not all made in France," he said, with authority. "This is called a Stanhope lens, after the third Lord Stanhope, the father of the famous Lady Hester who went off and lived like an Arab queen in the Lebanon."

"But surely that was long before Queen Victoria's time? I've never seen a peepshow souvenir which looked earlier than about 1870."

"No, you wouldn't. Lord Stanhope invented the microscopic lens, but the first microphotographs were taken in 1839 by a man in Manchester called Dancer. They weren't very successful until someone else invented the wet-plate process in 1851, but Dancer has the best claim to being the 'father' of modern micro-copying systems. Do you realise that it's possible now to microprint a hundred pages of text in the space of a page of ordinary print?"

"I know museums and libraries microfilm newspapers and documents to save space in their archives, and to duplicate priceless originals. But somehow I hadn't connected modern microfilming with Victorian peepshow souvenirs," said Imelda. "How did you come to find out all this?"

"While I was researching the Franco-Prussian War and the siege of Paris."

"Researching?"

136

Was it only her imagination, or had he, for a fraction of a second, the look of someone caught by a slip of the tongue?

"Reading about," he corrected himself, rather curtly. "As you probably know, Paris was besieged by the Prussians for nearly five months, and at first the only way the French inside could contact the French outside was by balloon. Because of the prevailing winds, it was only a one-way contact, so next they tried sending out a balloon full of racing pigeons. The snag with that idea was that ordinary despatches were so heavy that most of the three hundred pigeons were either shot down by Prussian guns, or caught by Prussian-trained falcons."

He paused. Thinking he had detected that she was still wondering why he had used the word "researched", she said hastily, "Poor birds! What happened then?"

"Someone thought of René Dagron. He had started out as a portrait photographer, but then he had seen the commercial possibilities of microphotographs in the form of souvenir fancy goods like this" – waving the paper-knife. "The French Government gave him a contract to organise a microscopic despatch service. He had to escape from Paris first, which he did; and then he was able to reduce the necessary despatches to about the size of a matchbox label, and eighteen of them could be fitted in a glass tube. Attached to a pigeon's tail, the tube didn't slow down its speed, or make it reduce its flying height. After the war, Dagron was asked to photograph all the records of a French insurance company. So even in 1871, they were beginning to see the scope of the thing."

"That's fascinating," said Imelda. "I've changed my mind. I shan't put that paper-knife in the shop. I'll keep it, and start a collection of peepshow souvenirs."

Charles replaced the knife on the table. "I didn't come

here to give you a lecture on French history," he said. "I wanted to ask a favour of you, Imelda."

"A favour?"

He studied her face for some moments, his own expression grave and very searching. "Perhaps 'favour' is too light a word. It may be too much to expect of you."

"I shouldn't think so. What is it?"

"Would you close the shop for a fortnight, and go to Menorca for me?"

CHAPTER V

"Go to Menorca?" she echoed, taken aback.

"My aunt has had to cut short her holiday. Her mother-in-law has had an accident, and there's no one else to look after her invalid father-in-law while his wife is in hospital. I had a cable from Menorca this afternoon. My aunt is already on her way back to England, which means that my grandmother is alone with the children."

He paused, his dark eyebrows contracted. "I have an important engagement in London at the end of the week after next. I don't want to cancel it, but I would do so rather than leave her alone out there. A possible compromise is to find someone willing to hold the fort until I'm clear of commitments. Naturally I thought of you."

"Naturally?" Imelda repeated, with an interrogative inflection. "Why me? Why not . . . Beatrix?"

His face took on a peculiarly enigmatic expression. "My grandmother doesn't like Beatrix. She does like you." Again he paused. "I realise it's a great deal to ask, but you haven't mentioned any holiday plans of your own and I should think you could do with a break. You've had a taxing year; changing your whole way of life, and launching a business."

Imelda was still too astounded to collect her thoughts and, misinterpreting her silence, Charles added, "If you're worrying about possible expenses – don't! A holiday at Na Vell doesn't call for a stack of new clothes, and my proposition naturally includes all your travelling expenses. I would run you down to Gatwick in the car, and as far as the flight is concerned there are several char-

139

ter schemes which allow the owners of houses in the Mediterranean to fly themselves and their families there and back at very cheap rates."

"But I'm not a member of your family."

"The scheme to which I subscribe is fairly elastic on that point. It includes fiancées, girl-friends, and au pairs. You wouldn't object to being listed as my girl-friend, would you?"

The seriousness with which he had been discussing the subject was leavened by a lurking glint of mockery.

"Wouldn't 'grandmother's help' be more accurate?" Imelda replied. "But aren't all charter flights fully booked during the high season?"

"Yes, but there are generally some last-minute cancellations, and I daresay I can pull a few strings. I was at school with the managing director of this airline."

"When would you want to go? Immediately, I suppose? Tomorrow, if possible?"

"Tomorrow would be ideal, assuming I can get you a seat on the flight. But can you be ready as soon as that?"

"I don't see why not. You say I shan't need many clothes."

"No, once you're accustomed to the sun you'll need only a bathing suit. Even Mahon, the island's capital, is only a small market town. The locals dress up for the evening *paseo* in the main square, and one sees some extraordinary rigs on tourists drinking in the pavement café of the American Bar. But most of the people with summer houses avoid Mahon when it's crowded. You could take one respectable dress, but you won't need more than one."

"Have you any idea what time we should have to set out tomorrow?"

"About eight o'clock, unless the flights have been retimed, which is unlikely." He rose to his feet. "I'd better be off. I have several telephone calls to make, and no doubt you will want to explain the situation to your people." He moved to the door. "Are you never nervous on your own here?"

"I might be jumpy in an isolated country cottage, but not here at the heart of the village. I can't help thinking of it as a village, even if, officially, it is a town."

"Nevertheless you're wise to keep a chain on your door after dark. Elderly people and women on their own can't be too careful these days. Goodnight, Imelda – and thank you for coming to the rescue."

"Goodnight, Charles." As she closed the door after him, she remembered thinking earlier on that his departure would leave her in a turmoil again. She had not envisaged such a turmoil!

Mrs. Dereham, when she heard what had happened, said, "But this is marvellous news, Melly. A fortnight in the sun with nothing to do but swim and keep an eye on the children will do you the world of good, darling. You were looking rather peaky when you came home. I think opening the shop has been more of a strain than you realise."

"Perhaps," Imelda agreed, glad that her mother had no inkling of the much greater strain of loving an unsuitable man.

"The Wingfields must think a lot of you to suggest such a thing," went on her mother. "Don't lose your heart to any of the island Don Juans, will you?" – laughing. "We don't mind you living in Norfolk, but Menorca is rather too remote."

After the telephone call to London, Imelda glanced at her watch. It was nearly ten o'clock. After some moments of indecision, she put on her raincoat and went to get the car out.

Although she knew the road in which Sam lived, she did not know the number of his parents' house. However, he had told her that for lack of a garage he left his van in the street at night. Unless he had gone out for the evening, the van would show her where to find him.

To her relief he was at home. But although the van, and a car which presumably belonged to his father, were parked outside the unkempt privet hedge of No. 17, there were no lights showing in the sitting-room or the front bedroom.

As Imelda followed the cement path which led along the side of the house, she heard the first sounds of the row, and when she turned the corner and approached the back door the volume of noise increased. At first she thought there were several people involved, and then she realised that one contributor to the uproar was a television disc jockey.

In other circumstances, she would have postponed her call. But this was an errand which could not be put off. She braced herself, and rapped loudly on the door.

At once there was silence within, apart from the background of too-loud "pop" music. A few seconds later the door was flung open by an angry-looking woman whom Imelda took to be Sam's mother.

"Mrs. Mutford? I'm Imelda Calthorpe. I'm sorry to disturb you at this hour, but could I have a word with Sam, please?"

Mrs. Mutford's grim expression gave place to surprise and curiosity. "He's upstairs. You'd better come in," she suggested ungraciously, and with no apparent embarrassment at finding that her high-pitched abuse had been overheard by a stranger.

The back door opened into a kitchen which adjoined a living room in a state of disorder which made Imelda

142

wonder how any woman could bear to live in such a muddle. Mr. Mutford was slumped in a chair, glowering at a large colour television. He glanced sourly at their visitor, and acknowledged her "Good evening" with a jerk of his head before returning his attention to the screen.

The house was evidently one of those in which the staircase ran up between the walls of the front and back rooms. Mrs. Mutford opened the inner door, and screamed up the stairs, "Sam! Sam! There's a young lady come to see you!"

She then returned to the room, and lit a cigarette, eyeing Imelda through the jets of smoke she exhaled from her nostrils. She did not ask her to sit down, and indeed there was nowhere to sit as Mr. Mutford was occupying the only armchair, and the upright chairs round the table bore piles of unironed washing, old newspapers, discarded clothing and other clutter. The table itself had not been cleared for some time, possibly not since breakfast, if a packet of cereal and an empty milk bottle had any significance. Probably they did not, Imelda reflected. It seemed the sort of household where cereal might be part of any and every meal to save the bother of preparing more troublesome fare.

She did not have to submit to Mrs. Mutford's scrutiny for long. In less than two minutes after his mother's bawled announcement, Sam hurried downstairs.

"What's up? Something wrong?" he demanded.

Imelda shook her head. "No – merely something unexpected which I wanted to tell you about."

Seeing that, once his first thought that she might be in trouble had been allayed, he was embarrassed about her seeing the condition of his home and hearing the violent altercation which had been in progress some minutes earlier, she added quickly, "Perhaps we could talk in the car.

143

I don't want to interrupt your father's programme."

"Good idea." In his desire to escape from the causes of his chagrin, Sam almost hustled her out of the house. "I suppose you heard the slanging match," he said bitterly, following her down the path.

"Most people have a row now and then, and they wouldn't expect a caller at this time of night," Imelda said matter-of-factly. "Sam, I have to go away for a fortnight. What I'm wondering is whether you would be willing to run the shop during my absence?"

They were facing each other across the roof of her car as she put the question, and before he could answer she opened the driver's door and ducked into her seat behind the wheel.

"You mean you'd leave me in charge of your place?" he demanded, as he slid in beside her. "After what you've just seen and heard in there?" – with a jerk of his head towards the house.

"What has that to do with it?"

"It was enough to put Diane off, and she's no one special compared with you. That old girl at the Hall who collects sewing stuff would never ask *her* to a dinner party."

"Mrs. Wingfield? I expect she would if Diane happened to be a fellow collector. When people share an enthusiasm it overcomes any other barriers between them."

He turned to her. "Does it, Imelda? Do you really believe that?"

There was a note in his voice which made her say hurriedly, "You wouldn't be tied to the shop all the time, because I'm sure Mrs. Walsham would be willing to mind it every morning."

Sam gave a deprecatory snort. "I wouldn't need her help. I can't stick her. She never stops nattering."

"Only because she has no one to talk to at home now.

I can't *not* ask her, Sam. She would be hurt. But I would make it quite clear that you had the final responsibility because you're also in the trade."

"Why do you have to go away? Has your mother been taken queer?" he asked.

The Norfolk turn of speech no longer sounded strange to her. "No, as it happens it's old Mrs. Wingfield who needs me. She's on holiday in Spain with the grandchildren. Her daughter, who was with them, has had to come back to England to deal with an emergency, and Mrs. Wingfield is getting on in years to cope with three children single-handed."

Sam's response to this explanation was to stare at his knees in brooding silence for some moments. At length, he said, "Okay, I'll look after the business for you."

"Oh, Sam, I am grateful. I don't –"

She broke off with a startled gasp as he put his arms round her and kissed her.

It was a shock; yet not a shock. She had been expecting it to happen for some time, but hoping that it would not. Now that it had, the best she could do was to submit without protest and hope that her lack of response would make Sam understand that she felt only friendship towards him.

"Oh . . . *hell*!" He let her go and sank back in his seat with a sort of despairing groan. His exclamation was obviously a substitute for a stronger expletive. He had always been touchingly careful never to swear when he was with her.

"I'm sorry, Sam," she said quietly. "I like you so much, but –" She left the sentence unfinished.

"But you don't fancy *him* as your father-in-law," he muttered with savage bitterness, his face turned towards his home.

"It has nothing to do with your family. Have you forgotten that *my* great-aunt was shunned for living in squalor, and thought to be soft in the head?"

"Being crazy is better than being stupid. Television and bingo are the only things which interest them. They don't want to know about anything else."

"Must you live with them? Couldn't you find a place of your own?"

"Maybe I'll do that." He shrugged, and said in a brisker tone, "When are you leaving? When d'you want me to take over?"

"Well, perhaps, in the circumstances, you may not wish —"

"Don't be daft! "

"If I could, I should like to leave at once. Tomorrow morning."

"Okay. Leave your keys with Bessie Medlar and don't worry about a thing. 'Night."

Before she had time to reply he had sprung out of the car and left her.

It was with a troubled mind that Imelda drove to the other side of the village to see her former landlady. As she had anticipated, Mrs. Walsham was willing to help, but would have preferred to mind the shop single-handed.

"Yes, but *I* shouldn't be at ease, leaving you at the mercy of any objectionable characters who might turn up. Who knows? Someone might try to sell you something which was hot. Sam is more likely to recognise a shady seller or a shoplifter."

"Oh, yes, I don't doubt *that*," replied Mrs. Walsham, with a meaningful sniff.

At which Imelda flared up and told her that the fact that she still disapproved of Sam was evidence of her poor judgment of character.

146

"He has *proved* what a good sort he is. I would trust him in any situation. Without his help, I doubt if Victoriana would even be open yet. So if you can't bring yourself to like him as much as I do, perhaps it would be best for *him* to manage the business single-handed," she ended hotly.

As soon as the hasty words were uttered, she regretted speaking so forcefully to someone of Mrs. Walsham's age and temperament.

Unexpectedly, the older woman did not take offence at Imelda's outburst. As she was seeing her to the door, she said, "You haven't an understanding with Sam, have you, dear?"

"No, there's nothing like that between us."

I almost wish there were, thought Imelda, as she climbed into the car and automatically clipped on the straps of the seat belt. Yet even if she loved Sam, their relationship would not be without some complications. Probably he would prefer to found his own business, even though it might be more rational to apply his energies to the one she had launched.

She had just finished putting the car away when from within the house she heard the telephone ringing. Quickly, she unlocked the door and hurried to lift the receiver before whoever was calling rang off.

"Have I dragged you out of a bath?" Charles asked, after she had given her number.

"No, no, it's all right. Could you hold on for a minute, please?"

She put the receiver carefully on the table, and went to close and bolt the back door which, in her haste, she had left open. "Sorry to keep you waiting," she said when she returned to the telephone.

"On the contrary it's I who should apologise for disturbing you so late." His voice, always attractive, sounded even more so by telephone. "I wanted to let you know that I've fixed up the flight to Menorca tomorrow and I've also arranged for you to fly from Norwich to Gatwick. A man I know runs an air-taxi service for businessmen. By a fortunate chance he's taking a couple of North Sea oil rig executives to Gatwick tomorrow morning and there's room for you. It will be much quicker and less tiring than going by road. Instead of setting out early you needn't leave home until ten-thirty."

"Oh ... marvellous!" Imelda replied, trying hard to inject some enthusiasm into her voice.

Her heart was sinking with disappointment at being denied the long drive alone with him. However tiring and boring the journey might have been for Charles, for her it would have been an interlude of unexpected happiness. By now she had reached the stage in love when merely to see him in the distance was better than nothing; to speak to him made a day memorable; and to spend several hours in his company was the nearest she was likely to come to bliss.

"You sound as if you might be having second thoughts," said Charles. "If you have changed your mind since I talked to you I hope you aren't afraid to say so."

"No, I haven't changed my mind. I'm about to pack my case."

"Don't stay up too late. See you in the morning. 'Night, Imelda."

"Good night, Charles."

Sam had been and gone and Mrs. Walsham was dusting the shelf of crested china when Charles came to fetch Imelda the following morning.

As he swung her suitcase inside the boot of his car

148

she felt another pang of regret for the journey they might have shared. To Norwich airport was a drive of less than half an hour.

"Is that little woman competent to hold the fort for you?" he asked as they set off and Imelda turned to wave.

"Not altogether, but Sam will be there most of the time."

She did not elaborate and Charles did not pursue the subject.

"Have you flown before?" he asked presently.

"No, never. I'm looking forward to it."

The airport was a comparatively new one. For a county where disused wartime airfields were a common sight Norfolk had been slow to accept the advantages of civil aviation.

Imelda, who had once been to London Airport not to fly but merely to have lunch, found this airport reassuringly small and homely compared with that vast and impersonal concourse.

Within a few minutes of their arrival Charles's friend appeared. He was introduced to Imelda and then the two men chatted until they were joined by the American oil men who had come by hired car from the coast. Shortly afterwards a stewardess came to shepherd the three passengers to the aircraft.

Imelda turned to Charles wondering if it was an appropriate moment to shake hands. Now at the very last moment she was beginning to feel slightly nervous. It would have been comforting to feel his firm warm grip for a few seconds.

While she was hesitating Charles took the initiative in a manner which effectively drove all thought of the hazards of take-off from her mind until long after they were airborne. He put his hands on her shoulders and bent down and kissed her on the mouth.

"Goodbye, my love. See you soon." With a friendly nod to the others, he turned away and strode out of the building.

Later that day Imelda realised that flying in a small twelve-seater aircraft was infinitely more interesting than jetting across the English Channel at an altitude which made freighters look like water beetles. But much of the interest of the first flight was wasted on her because all she could think of was Charles's extraordinary farewell.

Why had he done it? Not to bolster the impression that she was engaged to him because their relationship was irrelevant to the first flight and probably did not matter much in connection with the second one if he and the charter company's director were still close friends.

Could it be that he had detected her nervousness and kissed her to give her something else to think about? There had been amusement in his eyes when he looked down at her astonished face.

There was only one other possible explanation; and that she was afraid to let herself believe.

At Gatwick she was taken under the wing of John Brancaster, Charles's friend. She had lunch with him. He knew that she was a dealer and at first they talked about antiques. He was a collector of Staffordshire blue earthenware, specialising in plates depicting the adventures of Dr. Syntax, a comical clergyman drawn by Thomas Rowlandson, the eighteenth-century cartoonist.

Imelda won his approval by knowing that twenty-seven different illustrations had been documented of which John had so far collected twenty. Later however their conversation turned to Charles and in the course of reminiscing about their schooldays John remarked that

Charles had had a hard time as a boy because of his grandfather's unfair prejudice against him.

"Why was his grandfather prejudiced?" asked Imelda, unable to repress her curiosity.

"Charles hasn't told you? No, well, I suppose he wouldn't out of loyalty to old Mrs. Wingfield. He was always fond of his grandmother and she did her best to make matters easier for him. You see, Charles's grandfather never approved of his daughter-in-law. She was a foreigner: French or Italian, I'm not certain which. My parents met her once briefly, but before Charles was even at prep school she had married again and gone back to live in her own country."

"Leaving both her children here?" Imelda exclaimed incredulously.

"Yes; apparently the old man was right in his assessment of her character. She had married his son thinking she was on to a good thing. But when she found herself widowed and expected to live a quiet country life with two old people and two babies in a family which was not as well off as it had once been, she didn't care for the situation at all. I know the story only by hearsay, but I gather that old Mr. Wingfield wouldn't have minded if she had taken Charles abroad with her, but he wanted to bring up Piers himself. She wouldn't let him keep Piers unless he kept Charles as well."

"Ye gods! How completely callous of them both!" Imelda was wrung with pity.

"Yes, and the irony of the situation, although the old boy would never admit it, was that Charles looked like his mother but took after his father, and Piers was physically a thoroughbred Wingfield, but morally as selfish as his mother."

He paused to light a cigar, and went on, "Piers was sent to his father's school where he was damn nearly chucked out for doing something thoroughly disreputable. I don't know the details. Charles came to the third-rate school which was all my parents could afford, and he ended up as Head Boy with a string of prizes and scholarships. But even then his grandfather refused to acknowledge that he was worth ten of Piers."

"How did Charles and Piers get on with each other?"

"Surprisingly well, considering the difference between them. But as soon as Charles had come down from Cambridge – where he took a brilliant degree – he took off abroad. I believe he wrote to his grandmother, and occasionally I had a postcard from some remote part of the world. But until Piers was killed, and he had to come back and take the reins, Charles kept well away. Can you blame him?"

"Did you know what he did all that time? How he earned his living?"

John shook his head. "No, he always evaded my questions and after a time I took the hint and stopped pumping him. Maybe he went off the rails for a while. The way he was treated by the old man was enough to drive anyone to drink. Somehow, knowing Charles, I doubt if he sowed too many wild oats. It would be more like him to give up a flourishing career overseas to come back and fend for his brother's brood."

"I understood he was living in Menorca at the time of the accident. Would an island like that provide a good career for a foreigner?"

"Possibly not, although Charles speaks half a dozen languages, which would make it easier for him than for most people."

The second flight passed as quickly as the first, for now

Imelda was preoccupied by her lunch-table talk with John, and the new light it had thrown on Charles. No wonder he often seemed aloof. Such a boyhood was enough to make anyone reserved. Even if his grandmother had been fond of him, he must have suffered a great deal from his grandfather's hostility and the favouritism shown to his brother. It said a great deal for his character that, whatever bitter resentment he must have felt in the past, there was nothing but loving kindness in his attitude to the three children now in his charge. He might refuse them some things – she remembered the matter of the riding lessons – but he never withheld his time and interest.

Nevertheless, although he appeared to have survived his difficult boyhood without any lasting ill effects, she could not help wondering if when it came to relationships with women, he would always reserve his innermost self. She had read that when people had been deprived of affection in childhood it became impossible for them to establish satisfactory adult relationships. Thinking about this in connection with Charles, it seemed to her equally probable that the deficiencies of his early life might make him capable of a particularly strong and lasting love. But even with the feel of his kiss still on her lips, Imelda could not convince herself that she had the qualities to make Charles abandon the guards of a lifetime.

Her first sight of Menorca was from several thousand feet above the rocky coastline, indented here and there by small, secret-looking coves. The hinterland was a reddish-brown patchwork of fields enclosed by high dry-stone walls the colour of putty. There was very little vegetation, at least in the vicinity of the airport.

The small crowd awaiting the aeroplane's arrival were shaded from the dazzling glare of mid-afternoon by a lofty lattice of beams. Most of them were wearing sun-glasses, and at first Imelda could see only Spanish-looking people there. But as she entered the dappled light of the verandah area, she heard her name called and saw Henry grinning at her.

"Where are the others?" she asked, as he took charge of her one light suitcase.

"There's only me and Paco here. The girls have gone to a birthday party at Binibeca, and Granny has a head-ache, so she asked me to meet you. Did you enjoy the journey?" he asked politely.

"Yes, very much. It was cloudy over most of France, but I saw the peaks of the Pyrenees."

In the car park, Henry introduced Paco, a Menorquin youth who spoke no English. "He's Maria's son. Maria looks after Na Vell when it's empty," he explained.

For some miles after leaving the airport they drove along a main road and the countryside changed, becoming less flat and less barren. Then they turned up a narrow byroad flanked by the dry-stone walls which Imelda had noticed from the air. Presently the way was bar-red by a crudely made, sun-bleached gate. Paco stopped the car, and Henry hopped out to open the gate.

"Na Vell seems rather isolated," said Imelda, when they had passed through a second gate. "Are you on the telephone there?"

"I don't think there are any private telephones in Men-orca," the boy answered.

"What happens in an emergency? Say, if you needed to call a doctor quickly?"

"I suppose you would have to go to the nearest hotel. Perhaps the shops have telephones. I expect you're long-ing to have a swim, aren't you?"

Half an hour later Imelda was following him down a

154

gully leading to one of the secluded beaches she had glimpsed from the aircraft.

She had not yet seen Mrs. Wingfield as, on their arrival at Na Vell, Maria had hurried from the house to warn them by means of a graphic mime that the Señora was sleeping and should not be disturbed. Conducted by the island woman to a small, whitewashed shuttered bedroom, Imelda had obeyed Henry's behest to change at once into her swimsuit.

"You'll have to take care not to burn," he warned her, when they reached the hot sand where a couple of beach umbrellas provided shade for several loungers. "Granny was terrifically fussy about us when we first arrived. Have you brought some sun oil?"

"Yes," said Imelda, producing a bottle from her beach bag.

"When is Uncle Charles coming? It's much more fun when he's here."

"In about a fortnight, I think." While the boy ran down to the water's edge, she began to oil herself, wondering what Charles was doing now, and if already he had forgotten that teasing goodbye kiss.

The sea felt refreshingly cool when she waded up to her knees, but only by comparison with the furnace-heat of the afternoon air. When she had swum a few strokes she realised how warm the water was.

"Does no one else use this beach?" she asked Henry, when he swam alongside her while she was floating.

"It isn't private. Local people come here sometimes, but no other foreigners. It's a super place, isn't it?"

"Mm . . . lovely." Imelda rolled over and dived into the turquoise depths. She did not want to think about the fact that for her, as for Henry, the only thing lacking was Charles's presence; and that when he did join them, it

155

would be time for her to leave.

The sun had lost some of its fierceness when they climbed the hill to the house and found Mrs. Wingfield drinking coffee in the shadow of the east wall. Seeing Imelda, she rose to greet her with all her customary vitality.

"My dear child, how very nice to have you here! I do apologise for not being at the airport to meet you. I don't often suffer from headaches, but I had a blinding one earlier. My own fault probably. Too much wine and *chorizo* for supper last night. However, it's gone away now. Has Henry been a good host?"

"Yes, excellent. He's been teaching me to snorkel. Are you really feeling better, Mrs. Wingfield? I hope you haven't dragged yourself out of bed on my account?"

"No, no, I'm completely recovered. You must be thirsty after swimming. Henry, ask Maria to make a jug of iced orange juice, will you, please? Charles has put in a generator and we have a fridge and electric light and all the other mod. cons.," she explained to Imelda.

Shortly before sunset, Sophie and Fanny were brought home by the father of the child to whose party they had been. He lingered for a drink and a chat, and then jolted off down the walled lane in the direction of the lime-washed farm to which Maria had returned an hour before.

The proximity of the farm relieved a little of Imelda's anxiety at being several kilometres from the nearest tarred road, and heaven only knew how far from a telephone. Not that Mrs. Wingfield looked at all likely to be taken ill as she busied herself putting finishing touches to the supper largely prepared by Maria earlier in the day.

Later that night, when the children were in bed, their elders sat on the terrace which Charles had added to the seaward side of Na Vell.

"It is good of you to step into the breach now that Margaret has had to cut short her time here," said Mrs. Wingfield. "The children are so full of energy, but mine is waning, I'm sorry to say. There are times when I would rather sit quietly in the shade with my embroidery than scramble about on the cliffs as the young things naturally long to do. Does a hot climate suit you, Imelda?"

"I don't know, never having been abroad until now. We couldn't afford proper holidays after my father died."

In the days that followed, Imelda found that not only the heat but everything about the island suited her.

She liked getting up at first light to play badminton with Henry. She liked the toffee-tasting marmalade called angel's hair which they spread on crusty rolls baked in an old-fashioned wall oven and deliciously different from the steamed, sliced, tasteless factory product on which she had been brought up. She liked coming out of the clear green sea and lying on a towel on the sand under a sun which in minutes would evaporate the beads of salt water from her gently browning skin. She liked dozing in the shuttered half-light of her room during the hour's *siesta* which Mrs. Wingfield insisted upon after lunch.

By the end of the first week she was sufficiently tanned to spend all but the hottest hours of noonday with no other covering than her swimsuit. One afternoon when the children had gone with Paco to Alayor, a small inland town where they could spend their pocket money on packets of dried sunflower seeds, coconut ices and other delights not to be had at home in England, Imelda was sunbathing in solitude when someone addressed her in Spanish.

Startled, she opened her eyes to find Charles standing over her.

"*Charles*! What are you doing here?" she exclaimed, in amazement.

"I was able to get away sooner than I anticipated. How are you?" he asked, as she scrambled to her feet.

"Fine . . . how are you?" She knew that she was beaming from ear to ear, but she couldn't help it. It was such a lovely shock to see him.

"Hot and dusty," Charles said, with a grimace. "I arrived on the two o'clock flight, caught the Ciudadela bus to the turn-off, and walked the rest of the way. Where are the *niños*?"

This was one word she did understand. "They've gone to Alayor, and Maria has taken your grandmother to a house where they have some embroideries which have been handed down from the time of the British occupation. At least we *think* that is what Maria was telling us. Have you had any lunch? I'll come up to the house and fix you something."

"The first thing I need is a shower, and some different clothes. As you can see, I spent yesterday and this morning in London" – glancing down at the well-cut dark trousers which obviously belonged to a city suit. "And now" – transferring his glance to Imelda's scanty cotton coverings – "I feel decidedly over-dressed."

Twenty minutes later he came into the kitchen looking clean and cool in white sailcloth shorts and an apple green cotton-knit shirt which contrived to make him look as much a Menorquin as, down on the beach, he had sounded when he first spoke to her.

"How unfair! You're browner than I am before you've even started sunbathing," Imelda complained, comparing the light golden brown of her rounded forearm with the deeper tan of his sinewy one. For Charles, divested of English clothes, was unexpectedly powerful-looking.

He bent to look in the refrigerator. "Ah – *boquerones*!" He took out a covered plastic bowl, and helped himself to an anchovy pickled in brine. "Do you like these?" – offering the bowl to her.

Imelda nodded, and took one. "I'm rapidly becoming an addict. But the bread is my most serious weakness. I'm putting on pounds."

"If you are, it's entirely becoming," said Charles, with a glint in his eyes.

She remembered the manner of their parting, and said rather breathlessly, "Will you have your salad on the terrace?"

Presently, eating his lunch, he said, "You haven't asked how they're getting on at the shop."

Victoriana, Imelda realised, had hardly entered her head since her arrival, and certainly not since he had appeared on the scene.

She said lightly, "I expect you would have mentioned it if the shop had burned down or anything."

"I have a couple of notes for you from your caretakers. They're in my grip." He went to fetch them.

When he returned, Imelda said, "Now that you're here, there's no need for me to stay on."

"Do you want to hurry home?"

"No, but –"

"Then why do so?"

"For one thing, there isn't room for me. Where are you going to sleep?"

"On the camp bed out here, which is where I should sleep from choice at this time of year even if Na Vell were empty." He turned his head, listening to the clatter of hooves coming up the stony lane. "We have visitors."

But it was only Mrs. Wingfield and Maria, coming

159

home in the two-seater mule cart with its folding, perambulator-style hood.

At the sight of Charles, Maria gave a screech of pleasure, and launched into a voluble conversation.

"Such fun, Imelda," said Mrs. Wingfield. "I've always wanted to ride in one of these carts and the embroideries *were* what I hoped. Two beautiful eighteenth-century men's waistcoats and an early Georgian silk apron. By some miracle they've been carefully looked after all these years. There's no sign of damage from the mildew which Charles tells me is such a problem here in the winter months."

It was only when Maria had departed that Mrs. Wingfield was able to question her grandson about his unexpected arrival.

"That's splendid," she said, at the end of his brief explanation. "Now Imelda will be able to see something of the island's night life. Her first week here has been far too dull and quiet for what's supposed to be a holiday."

"I haven't been bored," Imelda protested.

"No, I know you haven't, my dear. You're too intelligent to be bored anywhere," said the older woman warmly. "But that doesn't mean that you couldn't have enjoyed yourself *more* had there been someone to take you about in the evenings. Now that Charles is here you can see some flamenco dancing at the open-air night club at San Luis. I forget the name of it" – with an interrogative glance at her grandson.

"Sa Tanca." It was impossible to judge from his expression what he thought about this suggestion.

"I expect Charles has a long list of Spanish girls with far better claims to his company than I have," Imelda remarked, hoping she sounded pleasantly off-hand.

At that his eyes narrowed mockingly. "Spanish girls
160

are still comparatively sheltered, particularly from Englishmen who have the reputation of being most dangerous escorts for well-brought-up *señoritas*," he said sardonically. "If I want to take a girl to Sa Tanca, I must find one of my own nationality who will either welcome my advances or at least know how to repel them."

"I'm afraid there's some truth in what Charles says," agreed his grandmother. "The English do have rather a bad reputation here. The retired people of my generation are reputed to drink far too much – as indeed some of them do – and the young girls who come on cheap package holidays are a magnet for the island youths who've read about our permissive society, and who hope to behave in a way which would never enter their heads with a Spanish girl."

"No doubt it enters their heads," said Charles dryly. The sound of an approaching motor made him add, "That sounds like Paco bringing the kids home." He drained his wineglass, and went to meet the car, whistling softly.

"Charles seems pleased with life," said Mrs. Wingfield. "He's always been rather self-contained and it's difficult to read his mind, but I think he has been depressed lately. Perhaps the political situation worries him. But today he looks altogether more cheerful even after that long, hot walk from the highway. It will do him good to have a rest from all the bills and Ministry forms. There was never all this wretched paperwork in my husband's time. Sometimes it keeps Charles at his desk until midnight, you know."

Presently Imelda went to her room to read the two letters Charles had brought from England.

"We're managing very nicely, so there's no need for you to worry," Mrs. Walsham had written.

Reading Sam's letter reminded Imelda of the incident in her car the night she had gone to his house. He made no reference to what had happened, but it troubled her to realise that she had not given it a thought since leaving England. Charles's casual kiss at the airport had erased Sam's embrace from her mind, and she felt ashamed of allowing her own emotional problems to obsess her to the point of forgetting the man who had been so good to her, and without whose help she would not be here on this idyllic island.

That night, leaving Maria to baby-sit, Charles took Mrs. Wingfield and Imelda to dine at a waterfront restaurant in Villacarlos, a small town on the brink of the huge, hill-sheltered harbour at the eastern end of the island.

The restaurant did not cater to tourists but to local people, and the adjoining bar was crowded with young Spanish soldiers from the nearby barracks. For the first time since her arrival Imelda found herself the target for a dozen or more fiery stares.

Mrs. Wingfield was walking ahead of her, and Charles was behind because he had held open the door. But he must have guessed that Imelda was taken aback by the barrage of attention focussed on her.

"You'll get used to it," he murmured in her ear.

The restaurant was a long narrow room with a paved floor, old bentwood chairs and painted walls decorated with advertisements for Xorigeur gin, San Miguel beer and Soberano brandy. But the food made up for the lack of elegance, although Imelda's enjoyment of her *canelones* was not enhanced by the stares of the four young men at the next table. She tried not to take any notice, but it was difficult to ignore such blatant attention. Anyone would think they had never seen a girl before, she thought, feeling more irked than flattered. Even when the centre of

162

their table was occupied by a large bowl of glistening purple-black mussels, they continued to shoot burning looks at her.

After dinner, they strolled along the moonlit quay, and Charles said, "Do you dislike the Spanish approach to women? I noticed you seemed rather restless during dinner. But if I'd told those four boys not to stare, they would have been surprised and affronted. Spanish girls are accustomed to being ogled. They think nothing of it."

"Well, I realise it doesn't mean anything. But I do think it's rather uncomfortable if one can't ever catch a male eye without receiving a leer like . . . like a flame-thrower!" she answered. "I'm glad it's not the custom in England."

Charles laughed. "I spent last night with some Spanish friends of mine who live in London. Their daughter was complaining to me that Englishmen look uninterested, and then suddenly something like this happens . . ."

He slid his hand around her waist and she felt his mouth brush her neck.

". . . which a Spaniard would never dream of doing without considerable encouragement," he added blandly, as his grandmother, some yards ahead, turned to remark that the waterfront cats seemed uncommonly nervous little creatures.

Later, sitting in the back of the car on the drive back to Na Vell, Imelda wondered how long it would be before Charles kissed her properly. She felt certain he intended to do so sooner or later. What she could not tell was whether he was playing with her, or serious.

In the days that followed, although he had several opportunities to do so, he did not touch her except in the most casual fashion.

He took them to picnic on Monte Toro, and while they

were scrambling about with the children he pulled her up a steep pitch of rockface. One morning, on a trip to Ciudadela, the city at the western end of the island, he grabbed her elbow to stop her jay-walking. And when she slipped playing badminton, and grazed her knee, Charles cleaned out the grit and dressed the place.

But as the warm silver nights followed the blue and gold days, he made no attempt to make love to her, although they were quite often alone together.

On the fourth day after his arrival, it was decided that they would all go to Mahon, the island's capital. Mrs. Wingfield wanted to buy shoes. The children wanted sweets, and postcards to send home to Mr. and Mrs. Betts. Charles wanted to visit the fish and provision markets, and the *bodega* where he bought wine.

"Would you care to look at the local junk shop while we're in Mahon?" he asked Imelda.

"Oh, is there one? I thought in Spain there were two extremes only; the very grand shop selling almost priceless art treasures, and tourist traps full of plastic armour and repro thumbscrews."

"There's some truth in that on the mainland, and the island has its share of plastic rubbish in the tourist season. But as in England, or anywhere, the best hunting grounds are tucked away in side-streets or villages. The place where I've picked up most of my things is not found by many holidaymakers."

"You didn't buy that in Menorca, surely?" She looked at a wall plate with a border of flowers, and the legend – *Himmlisch lächelt mir die Au, denk ich dich als meine Frau.*

"No, that was given to me in Switzerland."

"What do the words mean?"

They were momentarily alone in the living-room. With-

164

out looking at the plate, his eyes fixed on her face, he said, "They mean 'The meadows seem like the fields of heaven when I think that you may be my wife'."

If she had been in any doubt about her feelings for him, the effect of his translation would have convinced her.

But as Charles was about to say something else, Henry came into the room, followed by Maria who had something to say to Charles in Spanish.

As matters turned out, they did not go to the junk shop. They were on their way there when Charles met a man who insisted that they all had a drink with him in a pavement café on the Explanada, and who also invited Charles and Imelda to a party he was giving that night.

By the time the adults had finished chatting, and the children had been summoned from the swings in the Explanada gardens, everyone had had enough of the city — even a city in miniature such as Mahon — and were eager to get back to the beach.

It was after nine o'clock that night when Charles and Imelda set out for the party which was being held at a former farmhouse, now a country club on one of the new *urbanizacions* in which their host had an interest.

Charles did not talk much on the way, and Imelda was content to share his silence. The lights of isolated farms showed here and there in the folds of the starlit hills, and even on the main highway there was very little traffic. By the time they returned there would be less, and none on the byroad to Na Vell. When Charles had to stop to open the cattle gate, would he . . .?

She felt her throat tighten, and quickly switched her thoughts to the party, hoping her dress would be suitable. She had bought it in Ciudadela to set off her tan. It was white, with a narrow emerald belt.

From the moment they entered the club house the evening began to go wrong. At Na Vell, Charles had a tape recorder on which he played cassettes of Spanish guitar music, and the haunting *cante jondo* of Andalusia. Here, at the club, the music was a tuneless blare of pop. It was crowded and most people were smoking, which soon made Imelda's eyes smart. This was one of the reasons why, later, when Felix suggested a stroll to the *era* and back, she agreed.

The *era* was a circular threshing floor. She had noticed several about the countryside. Felix planned to convert this one to a dance floor. While he was telling her his plans for other improvements, he began to fondle her shoulders. Imelda was dumbfounded. He was old enough to be her father and surely he couldn't imagine that he was capable of cutting Charles out? Not that Charles had taken much notice of her in the past hour, she thought forlornly. He had been annexed – not unwillingly, it seemed – by a tall Nordic blonde who had shrieked with joy at the sight of him, and kissed him on both cheeks. They were evidently old friends, possibly more than friends, Imelda had thought, watching them dance together.

Had Felix been a contemporary, she would have rebuffed him unequivocally. Because he was middle-aged, she tried to deal with him tactfully. It was an error of judgment which resulted in an embarrassing tussle from which she emerged more exasperated than angry.

When, tidied and composed, she came out of the cloakroom to look for Charles, he and Birgitta seemed to have gone for a stroll.

Imelda had no intention of looking lost till he came back. When a Spaniard asked her to dance she pinned on a smile and was smiling with undiminished brightness when Charles reappeared.

"Oh hello, Charles. Have you met Jaime?" she asked, as he came to her side. Birgitta was no longer with him.

He responded to the introduction civilly enough, but then, taking the glass of wine from her hand and placing it firmly on the nearest horizontal surface, he said, "You must excuse us, *señor*. We have to leave early."

Gripping Imelda by the elbow, he marched her outside to where the car was parked.

CHAPTER VI

THEY were half way back to Na Vell before, unable to bear the silence a moment longer, she said, "I really don't see why *you* should look like a thundercloud. It may interest you to know that while you were chatting up your Swede, or whatever she is. I was fending off your horrible friend Felix."

She felt him ease off the throttle, and thought he was going to stop the car. But he changed his mind, and the needle crept back to his cruising speed. "If you were as skittish with Felix as you were with Jaime, I'm not surprised," said Charles, in an arctic tone.

"I was not being *skittish* with either of them," Imelda retorted furiously. "If anyone was being skittish, it was your friend Birgitta. No doubt she enjoys being taken to see the *era*."

He said nothing to this, but after some moments he gave a rather harsh laugh, and she sensed that his anger was cooling. Nevertheless he said nothing else until they reached Na Vell, and Imelda was not prepared to break the silence a second time.

When the car came to a standstill, she did not wait for Charles to come round to her side, but climbed out unaided. However, the handle of the door was an awkward one, and by the time she had opened it and was on her feet, Charles was there, one hand on the top of the door the other on the roof of the car so that, short of ducking under his arm, she was trapped between him and the Renault.

"So you were jealous of Birgitta." There was no mistaking his amusement. The moonlight fell full on his face revealing the laughter in his eyes, the smile on his lips. "You had no need to be."

"*No!*" Imelda's exclamation was an involuntary reaction to his movement to take her in his arms.

Ignoring her objection, Charles drew her firmly against him.

It was not until some time later, when she was lying on her bed staring at the pattern of silver bars made by the moonlight slanting through the slats of the shutters, that Imelda began to regret wrenching free from his arms and running indoors.

Her flight from him had been instinctive. She had felt that he could only be playing with her, and when her own emotions were so much more deeply engaged, she could not bear to be kissed merely as a diversion.

The following day was a nightmare of constraint. It began when Mrs. Wingfield asked at breakfast, "Was it a good party?"

"Yes . . . very," Imelda answered hollowly.

"Unforgettable," Charles added sardonically.

Fortunately neither his grandmother nor the children seemed to notice any difference in his manner. But Imelda was continually aware of the derision in his eyes, and of the studied way he stepped back much further than was necessary if they happened to meet in a doorway or going up and down the beach path.

He spent the evening immersed in a book while his grandmother did her embroidery and chatted to Imelda who, at Mrs. Wingfield's suggestion, was trying her hand at some stitches on a spare scrap of canvas.

"I think I might adapt the motifs on that wall plate for use on a cloth and a set of napkins," said Mrs. Wingfield, after a discourse on design to which Imelda had listened with less than her usual attention.

Imelda glanced at the Swiss plate, and the meaning of the words and the tone in which Charles had translated them made her regret even more bitterly her hasty action the night before. All day there had been growing in her the feeling that perhaps she had misjudged him and, in doing so, had blighted something irreplaceable. But if she had mistaken his motive, how was she to retrieve her error? There seemed no way at all.

"Charles is very badly off for decent table linen here," his grandmother went on, pursuing her very different train of thought.

The mention of his name made Charles look up from his book, first at his grandmother whose attention was now engaged on the threading of her needle, and then at Imelda who did not have time to switch her gaze from his face.

For a long moment, their eyes met. In hers, she hoped, he would read an appeal for the resumption of the easy relationship they had enjoyed before the party. In his she could see nothing but indifference.

"I – I have a slight headache. I think, if you don't mind, I'll go to bed early," she said, in a low voice to Mrs. Wingfield.

"Yes, I should. Have you some aspirins with you? If not –"

"I have some, thank you. Goodnight." For the benefit of Mrs. Wingfield, she added, "Goodnight, Charles."

To her surprise he was already on his feet. As he opened the door for her he said, "Imelda –"

"Yes?" She kept her eyes down so that he should not see the foolish tears in them.

170

"I hope you feel better in the morning." His tone could not have been more coldly courteous. "Goodnight."

The next day promised to be the same, but shortly before noon Henry came pelting down to the beach to announce excitedly that the Guardia had come to the house and Maria was having hysterics.

"What the devil . . .?" exclaimed Charles, rising to his feet.

"I think it has something to do with Imelda," said Henry. "The only word I understood was *señorita*, and they said it several times."

"In that case you'd better come with me, Imelda," said Charles, looking to where she was sitting up on her woven grass sunbathing mat.

"No, not you, children. We'll stay here," remarked Mrs. Wingfield firmly, seeing that they meant to follow their uncle.

"Oh, Granny, we want to see the Guardia," Sophie protested.

"Later, perhaps. Not just now."

Half way up the path to the house Imelda halted.

"What's the matter?" Charles asked from behind her.

She turned to him, her face stricken, their estrangement forgotten. "My family . . . could there have been a car accident? Would the Guardia bring that kind of news?"

He laid his hand on her shoulder, and tightened his fingers in a brief, firm grip of reassurance. "It may not be anything serious."

The policemen's motorbikes were propped side by side in the courtyard, and they and Maria were in the sitting-room, all talking at once, when Charles arrived on the

171

scene. He quieted the island woman's melodramatic exclamations, and put a single curt question to the senior Guardia. The man replied, and Charles turned to Imelda. "None of your family has been hurt."

"Th – thank goodness for that," she said unsteadily.

"I should sit down if I were you." He held a short conversation in his easy idiomatic Spanish, and gave an instruction to Maria. Then he turned again to Imelda. "They've brought a message from Norfolk. There's been some trouble at the shop."

"What kind of trouble?"

"A fire. They have no information about the cause, but apparently the damage is fairly extensive, and it's advisable for you to return to England as soon as possible."

Maria reappeared with a bottle of Fundador and some glasses on a tray. The policemen took off their white crash helmets, and wiped their sticky foreheads. They wore breeches, with black leather Sam Browne belts and kneeboots. But the removal of their helmets made them look considerably less formidable.

"Have some brandy," advised Charles, putting a glass into Imelda's hand. "I'm going down to the beach to tell Grandmother what's happened. I shan't be gone for more than a minute or two. Don't worry: I'll help you to deal with everything."

When he had left them, Maria demonstrated her sympathy by making clucking noises and patting Imelda's hands. Then she turned to talk to the police, making frequent mentions of "Don Carlos" and "Señorita Imelda", but in what context Imelda was unable to guess.

Sipping the brandy Charles had given her, she was conscious not of distress at the bad news but of relief that it had put an end to the unbearable constraint between them.

By the time the others arrived, the Guardia were preparing to depart. As Charles had told her when he was talking about Menorquin customs, they left most of the brandy in their glasses, not because they were not supposed to drink while on duty, but because on an island where spirits were very cheap, it was considered courteous, not wasteful, to do so.

As the roar of their engines diminished, Mrs. Wingfield said, "This is very upsetting, my poor child. What can have happened, I wonder? Charles, isn't it possible to telephone Sergeant Saxtead and find out precisely what has occurred?"

"Yes, that's what I propose to do." He looked at his watch. "I wonder what chance we have of getting seats on an aircraft today, or tomorrow? It could be a week before there are any cancellations. That's the only drawback about an island. Without reservations, it can be almost impossible to leave Menorca during the tourist season."

"How long would it take you to motor back?" enquired his grandmother.

"Forty-eight hours, and Imelda would be exhausted when we arrived. Besides, the ferry to Barcelona is as heavily booked as the airlines, and even if it were not, I wouldn't be keen on doing that long fast run in a hired car. Somehow or other we must get ourselves on board an aircraft."

"But it isn't necessary for *you* to go back to England," said Imelda.

"My dear girl, you don't imagine that I'd let you go back alone? I didn't tell you everything at once. The fact is that the shop is completely burnt out, and both Mrs. Walsham and young Mutford are in hospital, suffering from burns. They're not on the critical list, but their injuries are not minor ones. I'm going along the cliffs to the

Hotel Alfonso Tres to make some telephone calls. I'll be back as soon as I can. Do you want to come, kids?"

While he and the children were gone, the two English-women discussed the bad news.

"What *could* have started it? All the wiring was renewed and checked before I moved in," said Imelda. "And neither Sam nor Mrs. Walsham smoke, so a cigar-ette end can't have caused it."

"Unless one of the customers dropped one, and Mrs. Walsham didn't notice it smouldering," said Mrs. Wing-field.

When Charles returned, two hours later, he was able to put an end to their conjectures. As the children had lunched at the hotel, they were sent to have their *siesta* and while the grown-ups had lunch, he told them the out-come of his telephone calls. Luckily there were four vac-ant seats on a package tour flight leaving Menorca at ten o'clock that evening, and landing at Gatwick at midnight.

"It's not one of John's aircraft, but I've been in touch with him and arranged for a car to be waiting for us," Charles explained. "We should be in Norwich by four – the roads will be clear at that hour – which will give Ime-lda time for a few hours' sleep before going to the hos-pital. When I spoke to Sergeant Saxtead, I asked him to tell Mr. and Mrs. Betts that we were on our way home and expected to arrive in the early hours."

"Did the sergeant tell you more about the fire?" asked his grandmother.

"Yes, it was caused by one of those deep fat pans for frying chips."

"But I haven't a chip pan," put in Imelda.

"Perhaps Mrs. Walsham has and took hers to the shop," suggested Mrs. Wingfield.

"I suppose that must be the explanation. But how very

unlike her to let the fat become so hot that it caught fire. She's not at all a careless person."

Charles said, "It seems she was called away from the kitchen soon after starting to heat the fat. When it ignited, instead of covering the pan, which would have smothered the flames, she panicked and rushed for help. She never reached the street because she tripped and fell, knocking herself out. Fortunately Sam Mutford turned up before the fire had spread beyond the kitchen. He carried her outside, called the Fire Brigade, and then dashed upstairs to save as many of your personal belongings as possible, Imelda. By the time the firemen arrived, the back of the house was an inferno and Mutford himself had to be rescued."

"So Mrs. Walsham wasn't burnt, as we first thought?" said his grandmother.

"No, merely concussed. She'll be discharged in a day or two."

Thus it was that at half past eight that evening Charles and Imelda were driven to the airport by Paco. But owing to some technical fault which was not explained in detail it was nearly one o'clock in the morning before the passengers were allowed to board the aircraft and three before they landed at Gatwick

The car organised for them by John Brancaster was not a self-drive one, as Imelda had expected. It was a large black limousine with uniformed chauffeur to drive it.

Charles apologised to the driver for keeping him waiting, and the man said he had been notified of the delay and had had a nap. Certainly he looked fully alert as he tucked a rug round Imelda. By this time she was exhausted and hardly able to keep her eyes open. She made an effort to stay awake until they had left the lights of the airport

175

behind. Then sleep could no longer be resisted.

When she woke, it was light, and they were passing through the centre of Norwich. Charles was telling the driver which road to take out of the city.

She had been so deeply asleep that it was a little while before she stirred. And before she reached that stage she discovered that she and Charles were no longer in different corners of the car, separated by several feet of opulent hide upholstery. They were both in the centre of the seat, and she was leaning against his chest, and his arm was round her waist. The surprise of this discovery almost made her jerk upright. Her heart began to pound so violently that it seemed he must feel it too. But apparently he didn't and she stayed where she was, pretending not to have woken, until they slowed down for the turn through the tall gateway to the Hall.

Then, as she was about to go through the motions of rousing, Charles gave her a gentle shake. "Wake up, Imelda. We're almost home."

For a few seconds longer she stayed in the shelter of his arm. Then she sat up and rubbed her eyes. As she did so he shifted his position so that, if she had been genuinely half awake, she might not have realised that she had been sleeping in the crook of his arm with her head on his shoulder.

But she did realise it, and she had made up her mind what she meant to do when the car reached the sweep in front of the house. And when they got there, she turned and looked Charles in the eyes, with her warmest smile. "You've been wonderful to me. Thank you." She leaned towards him and kissed his lean, sunburned cheek.

The answering expression in his eyes when she drew back to see his reaction made her absolutely certain that the reason he had come back to England with her was not

176

merely kindness. But he did not say anything because by then the car had stopped, and Mr. Betts was hurrying out to receive them.

Within a quarter of an hour of their arrival, Charles and Imelda and the driver were eating a substantial breakfast while Mr. and Mrs. Betts recounted everything they knew about the fire, and showed them the photographs which had appeared in the previous night's issue of the *Eastern Evening News*.

After breakfast, the driver set out on his return journey, and Charles fetched his own car from the garage and took Imelda to see what was left of Victoriana.

Even though the newspaper pictures had prepared her for the wreckage of her property, it was still a shock to see the charred shell of the building she had left in good order. What had not been destroyed by the fire had been ruined by the water necessary to extinguish the flames.

"Poor old Bessie. I hope the shock hasn't been too much for her," said Imelda as she tapped on Mrs. Medlar's door.

But the old lady was in high spirits. Once the danger to her own home had passed, she seemed to have enjoyed all the fuss. She held them captive for an hour while she gave them her own account of the conflagration.

"Well, that seems to have put paid to my career as a dealer," said Imelda, when they were driving to the hospital in Norwich. "I can't possibly afford to rebuild."

"You could sell the site and rent a shop."

"Yes, but where should I live? I don't much fancy digs again, having had a taste of independence."

He did not answer immediately. After a pause, he said, "I expect there's a solution to that problem. While you're visiting the casualties, I'll ponder it." He didn't take his eyes off the road, but when she glanced quickly at him she saw the ghost of a grin.

At the sight of her visitor, Mrs. Walsham began to cry. Imelda did her best to comfort her, but without much success. Nothing she could say would convince the little Londoner that what had happened was not an unforgivable disaster.

"Have you seen that poor boy yet?" Mrs. Walsham asked, in a quavering voice, when Imelda's repeated reassurances had staunched the flood to some extent.

"No, I'm going to visit Sam presently."

"If it hadn't been for him, I should have been burned to death," Mrs. Walsham exclaimed, with a shudder. "He saved my life, and I'm sure he must have known I didn't like him." She began to sob again.

It was a relief when the Sister came to put an end to the visit.

"It's unfortunate that this should have happened just when she was beginning to come to terms with the loss of her husband," said Imelda worriedly, as they walked away from the side ward.

"It's bad luck for you, having your shop wrecked, and your summer holiday spoiled," the Sister said sympathetically. "What a shame when you've only been open a short time. Those wretched chip pans are a menace!"

Sam was among a dozen or more patients in a large ward. He was lying with closed eyes when Imelda approached his bedside and, not wishing to wake him if he were sleeping, she hovered uncertainly by the footrail until the man in the neighbouring bed lowered the magazine he was reading and said, "Hey, Sam, there's a young lady to see you."

Immediately Sam's eyes opened. "Imelda! You got back quickly!" He made an attempt to sit up, but flinched and sagged against the pillows. His hands and forearms were swathed in dressings, and evidently the involuntary pressure on his elbows had caused him considerable pain. In spite of it, the sight of her lit a warmth in his eyes.

"Oh, Sam, fancy risking your life to save my worthless bits and pieces. I would rather have lost everything than have you hurt," she exclaimed.

"I'm not that badly hurt," he said cheerfully. "A bit singed here and there. Nothing to worry about. You look great, Imelda. A tan suits you. It's too bad you had to rush back. Have you seen the shop yet?"

She nodded. "We just came from there."

"We?"

"Charles Wingfield came back to England with me."

The light died out of Sam's eyes. "I see. That was decent of him. You'll need someone to help you deal with everything. How much of a write-off is the place? They hustled me off in an ambulance while it was still on fire, but there was a picture in the paper last night which made it look a total wreck."

"Yes, it is."

The man in the next bed remarked, "They say the mess from the water is as bad as the fire damage, more often than not."

He started to tell a long, detailed tale of a fire caused by an incendiary bomb during the second World War. Sam raised his eyes to the ceiling. In mid-anecdote, his fellow patient was cut short by a nurse who bustled up, announcing, "Time for your injection, Mr. Snape."

"Just my luck to be next to a natterer," murmured Sam, when Mr. Snape had been curtained off. "Pour me some water, would you, Imelda?"

She did so, and held the feeding cup to his lips. "Wouldn't you like something more interesting than water? You must let me do some shopping for you, Sam.

I'll organise some fruit and cheese and so forth. I daresay the food is fairly dull in here. It is in most institutions. High on stodge, low on protein."

"You mustn't trouble about me. You'll have your hands full sorting out the shop. How's the old girl? Have you seen her?"

"She's terribly upset."

"So she should be, silly woman. She's like Diane's mother; afraid to be seen coming out of the fish shop with a parcel of cod and five of chips."

Imelda smiled. "I don't think it's that. She prefers home-cooked chips, or rather she did before this happened. I doubt if she'll ever use a chip pan again."

Sam said, "What will you do? Have you decided yet? Will you pack up and go back to London?"

"I haven't begun to think about it. You and Mrs. Walsham are my first concern. Have they given you any idea how long you'll be here?"

"Only a few days. After that the district nurse will change the dressings for me. It'll be a couple of weeks before my hands are healed, I reckon."

Imelda thought a couple of months would be a more accurate estimate. Aloud, she said, "Poor Sam, I'm sure they're horribly painful, although you make light of it."

She spent half an hour with him, and then went out to buy the various things she felt he should have to make him more comfortable.

It was noon when she and Charles returned to the Hall, and by then she was longing for a bath and a change of clothes. When she joined Charles in the library, he said, "Lunch won't be ready for about half an hour, I'm afraid. I told Mrs. Betts we would take pot luck, but she hasn't taken me at my word. There's something special cooking. Sit down. You must be very tired."

"No, I don't feel at all tired – yet. I expect I may later on." Imelda seated herself by the open window and gazed at the garden so green after the arid landscape of the island. It was a fine summer's day, but compared with the heat of Menorca it seemed cool in spite of the sunlight.

Charles said, "This may seem a curious moment to embark on the story of my life, but if you can bear it I'd like to tell you one or two excerpts."

She turned faintly startled eyes towards him. But now he was contemplating the ivory cattle grazing in the parkland beyond the cedars.

"When I finished my education I hadn't decided what to do with my life," he began slowly. "My brother Piers was expected to follow my grandfather here and was happy to do so. I had no pre-selected role in life and apparently no métier either."

"But you were very clever," she said. "Your friend John told me that you had a brilliant career at school and at Cambridge."

"I had a facility for passing examinations," he said, with a shrug. "But I wasn't a born academic. I decided to put off the decision on what to do with myself, and knock about the world for a bit."

She sipped the sherry he had given her, and waited for him to continue. Now, sitting in this peaceful English room, listening to his quiet voice, it was hard to believe that the night before last she had fought her way out of his arms.

"For several years I took whatever work offered. Rough work, mostly, but it paid my way to the East and the South Pacific. Then I had a look at the Americas. Eventually I came back to Europe, and there I found my vocation." He glanced at her glass and saw it was empty. "More sherry?"

"Thank you." She was longing to ask him what vocation he had found, but she sensed that he wanted to tell the story in his own way.

Their glasses replenished, he sat down in the chair at the desk, turning it so that he faced her. Now, for the first time, he looked at her while he was talking instead of frowning abstractedly out of the window.

"I had bought Na Vell, and was living there in the spring and autumn, and working in various other places during the winter and summer, when Piers and Rowena were killed and I had to come back and become caretaker for Henry," he went on. "As far as I'm concerned, my present way of life is a temporary one. As soon as Henry is capable of taking the reins, I propose to let him get on with it, and revert to my chosen way of life."

He paused, still watching her intently. "I'm telling you this because I want to make it absolutely clear that all this" – with a gesture encompassing the huge room and spreading grounds outside it – "is not my life style. All I have of my own is Na Vell, and a small, earned income from one of the most insecure careers a man can choose."

He turned to place his glass on the desk. He had not finished the sherry, but he seemed suddenly to find the glass an encumbrance. With his hands on the arms of the chair, he said, "Now that you know how little I have to offer you, will you marry me, Imelda?"

In her daydreams never once had she envisaged this oddly formal proposal. She said in a quick, shaky voice, "Oh, Charles, you are a fool. Don't you know that if people love people they don't give a hoot about incomes and prospects and security?"

And then Charles was no longer in the chair, but holding her tight in his arms, so tight that she had to hold her

182

breath. "I wasn't entirely sure that people *did* love people," he said, close to her ear. "You've been such a sphinx lately, my love. I haven't known what you've been feeling – except the night before last when you seemed afraid of me and ran away."

This time she did not run away.

It seemed only a few moments later that the gong in the hall began to boom. "Oh, to hell with lunch," said Charles huskily.

But a few minutes later he released her, and they looked at each other with the dazed, smiling faces of people still in shock from unexpected joy.

"Mrs. Betts, we're engaged," Charles announced, when the housekeeper entered the dining-room to remove their pâté plates and serve the main course.

"Oh, Mr. Charles, I'm so glad – and so will your grandmother be. She's been hoping for this for a long time," Mrs. Betts said, beaming at them.

"Really?" Charles looked surprised. "She hasn't said so to me."

"Well, no, she hasn't *said* so to me. But I know it will please her, all the same. She's always been partial to Miss Calthorpe."

"After lunch, we'll send Grandmother a cable," said Charles, when they were alone again.

It was not until they were eating cheese and biscuits that Imelda said, "You still haven't told me what you did for a living, and will do again when you leave here."

"When *we* leave here," he corrected her. "That's something else I ought to have told you beforehand, I suppose. I haven't actually stopped doing my own work, but I haven't time during the day, so I have to do it at night."

"You mean when your grandmother thinks you're

struggling with the farm accounts you're actually doing something else?"

"Yes, she doesn't know about it. If she did, she would realise how uncongenial my daytime work is to me. And it's for her sake almost as much as Henry's that I'm here at all," answered Charles. "My grandfather and I were always rather at loggerheads, and she did a lot to smooth my path as a boy. So I feel I owe her some serenity in her old age. In fact I shan't be able to keep my secret much longer, because this was waiting for me when we arrived."

He took from his pocket an opened envelope, and handed it across the table to her.

The letter which Imelda unfolded was from the Secretary of the Royal Society of Literature, and it was an invitation for Charles to accept a Fellowship.

"You mean . . . you're a writer?"

"An historian," said Charles. "One of your favourite historians, so you once told me."

She looked blank for a moment. Then: "You can't mean *you* are D. G. Hepburn?" Her mind flashed back to the day she had come from a jumble sale with a copy of *Bayard*, a favourite book which had been too expensive for her to buy when it was first published.

"My full name is Charles David Guy Hepburn Wingfield. Is it a sad disillusionment?"

"No – a fantastic surprise. To be marrying D. G. Hepburn . . . I can't believe it!"

"Being a writer's wife is no picnic," he warned her seriously. "You're letting yourself in for some lonely evenings, I'm afraid."

"I shall ask your grandmother to teach me all she knows about embroidery. I shan't interfere with your work. I shall be too proud of it." She gave the letter back. "Will you be installed with great pomp?"

184

"No, it's quite an informal ceremony, I believe. One is introduced to the President, and one signs in with Byron's pen. Reading a paper to the Society comes later on."

"What are you writing now?"

"I've just finished a book about Richard Kane. He was a governor of Menorca during the British occupation who had a great deal of beneficial influence on the life of the island."

After lunch, they lounged in deck chairs in the garden, drowsily talking and planning. Now and then Charles would lean over to kiss her.

"Enough of my career. What about yours?" he said. "I was wondering if you would be satisfied with a stall in the Wednesday antique market at my grandmother's subscription library? Or is one day a week not enough? You would need another day to go about looking for stock, of course."

"Two days a week would be more than enough, I should think, if I'm going to relieve your grandmother of the things she has to do at present."

A frown contracted his dark brows. "It's a lot for you to take on; this great house and three ready-made children."

"The children are darlings. I'm very fond of them already. We could afford to have *one* more, couldn't we?"

His expression lightened into laughter. "I should think we might run to one more. Any ideas about where you'd like to go for a honeymoon?"

"I'll leave it to you. You know more places than I do."

"I should like to take you to the Jura Mountains, and perhaps further south to Dauphiné."

"That's where Bayard was born, isn't it? I suppose you went there for your book."

"Yes, and I've always wanted to go back and explore
185

that part of France more leisurely. The Jura is heavily forested with slow, winding rivers and small hillside towns where there's usually one comfortable *auberge* where the food and wine are first rate. The bedrooms are furnished with massive *armoires* and large double beds with feather *duvets*. Does that sort of place appeal to you, or would you rather go somewhere more lively?"

"The Jura sounds heavenly. But when? Were you thinking of next spring?"

"Next spring! Are you mad, girl? I was thinking of next month. Why should we delay until next spring? You don't want one of those elaborate weddings which take half a year to organise, do you?"

"Oh, no, not a bit," she said at once. "I'd much rather have a very quiet wedding like my mother's to Ben. But won't people expect *you* to have a traditional affair with a marquee and champagne and a photograph in *Country Life*? Somehow I had the impression that we should have to be married here in Norfolk rather than from my home."

"Piers and Rowena had a fashionable wedding," said Charles. "People will have to wait for the next one until young Henry finds himself a wife. I don't see marriage as an occasion for lavish public display but rather as something which ought to be as private as possible." A sudden flicker of amusement lit his eyes. "Do you remember the day I gave you a lift to Norwich to catch the London train?"

"Very clearly. I certainly never thought then that, before the year was out, we should be discussing our wedding. I disliked you more than any man I'd met," Imelda confessed, with a grin. "Charles, why did you look so annoyed when I said I couldn't see why you should be so concerned about my plans, except for the fact that you

186

didn't wish to fail Beatrix? You looked daggers at me, and said, 'What do you mean by that remark?' in your iciest voice."

"What *did* you mean by that remark?"

"I thought you were . . . involved with her."

"Beatrix was attracted by the idea of being Mrs. Wingfield. Thinking we have a great deal more money than is actually the case, she was prepared to put up with the children, and with me as a husband."

"I don't think she found *you* unattractive," Imelda said dryly.

He shrugged. "She wouldn't have wasted much charm on me had Piers been alive and unmarried."

"What was your brother's wife like?"

"Rowena?" Charles considered for a moment before he answered, but there was nothing in his expression to cause her the smallest prick of unease. And when he said, "Rowena was a nice-looking lass, but not very bright and with very little sense of humour," Imelda knew the impression she had formed had been a false one, like so many of her ideas about him.

"Charles, why, when we were both travelling back from London, did you more or less cut me? Was it because you thought Sam had been kissing me when you came to the shop a few days earlier?"

"I must admit that I didn't have very cordial feelings towards Sam at that time. But if I seemed to scowl at you at Liverpool Street, it was chiefly because I had just been caught by a particularly boring acquaintance when I had intended to spend the journey mulling over the notes I'd made at the Public Record Office. When the train reached Norwich I hoped to give you a lift home, but I couldn't see you."

"I was skulking in the 'ladies' to avoid you. How absurdly people behave when they're in love! Can you imagine any sane person hiding from the man they most want to see in all the world?"

"Were you in love at that stage?"

"I think so. It's difficult to be precise. Right from the beginning my feelings about you were very mixed. Even when I was furious with you for being so hostile and patronising the first night I stayed here, I remember thinking at breakfast that at least you were considerate with your household."

"What did I do to earn your grudging approval on that score?" he asked, amused.

"You went to the kitchen to tell Mrs. Betts I had come down, and you took the coffee pot with you instead of ringing for her to come to the dining-room and fetch it. I thought it was an indication that you weren't *entirely* selfish." She told him about the remarks she had overheard coming downstairs, and which had set her against him. "When did you begin to like me?"

"I liked the look of you when I saw you walking down the platform with my grandmother."

"You didn't behave in a friendly way. You could hardly have been more standoffish."

"Every time I was friendly, you froze. Why were you so unco-operative when I kissed you at Na Vell?"

"I thought you might be making love without actually loving. People do."

He said, "I had already declared my feelings, but I don't think you got the message."

"What message?"

"*Himmlisch lächelt mir die Au, denk ich als meine Frau.* The meadows seem like the fields of heaven when I think that you may be my wife ... that you *will* be my wife," Charles amended.

Golden Harlequin $1.95 per vol.

Each Volume Contains 3 Complete Harlequin Romances

Golden Harlequin $1.95 per vol.

Each Volume Contains 3 Complete Harlequin Romances

Volume 3

Volume 4

Golden Harlequin $1.95 per vol

Each Volume Contains 3 Complete Harlequin Romances

☐ Volume 5

LAKE OF SHADOWS by Jane Arbor   88

Kate had to give up her job in London and return to her Irish lakesid
home to care for an ailing father — so the man she hoped to marr
walked out on her.

MOON OVER THE ALPS by Essie Summers   86

Because of a disappointment in romance, Penny tried to make a ne
life in a remote sheep station in the New Zealand Alps. Unfortunate
it was the one place where this task would prove most difficult!

SHIPS SURGEON by Celine Conway   72

When Pat Fenley boarded the liner "Walhara" to take a young patier
to Ceylon, she didn't expect to find that the patient would be in grav
danger.

☐ Volume 6

A LONG WAY FROM HOME by Jane Fraser   81

From a lonely, windswept island in the Hebrides to a luxurious villo
in the Mediterranean. For Kate Kelsey this meant the prospect of o
life of luxury. But what about Jamie?

NEVER TO LOVE by Anne Weale   644

Andrea, a successful model determined to marry Justin for money and
security. But once free from financial worries, she began to realise
what it was like to live without love.

THE GOLDEN ROSE by Kathryn Blair   650

Once in Mozambique, Gwen finds herself opposing the autocratic
Duque de Condeiro whilst helping her uncle and his small motherless
son.